Pepped Up and Ready

(Pepper Jones Series, Book #3)

By Ali Dean

Editor: Leanne Rabesa

http://editingjuggernaut.wordpress.com

Cover: Sarah Foster

http://sprinklesontopstudios.com

Proof Reader: Nicole Bailey

http://proofbeforeyoupublish.com

Chapter 1

There's nothing like sprinting up a hill as fast as you can. Leaning forward and digging your feet into the dirt as you push your body to a point where all conscious thoughts escape your brain. You can't focus on anything except the burning in your chest and the urgency to reach the top.

It was still dark when I started jogging this morning, and the sky begins to turn from a hazy purple to a blend of red and orange as I reach the sign indicating the highest point on Duncan Peak. I burst past it with a final surge of energy before letting myself fall dramatically to the ground. I roll onto my back and grin, knowing there's no one in sight to witness my ridiculousness. It's just me and the mountain.

As my breathing settles and the sky colors change with the rising sun, a heaviness I'm growing accustomed to eases over me, pinning me to the ground. I don't want to get back up and face it. The weight of impending change.

The boy I've grown up with is going to college tomorrow. Jace Wilder is my boyfriend now, but saying "my boyfriend is going to college" just sounds so... trivial. Lots of girls experience that. Two of my best friends, Zoe Burton and Charlie Owens, have been dating for even longer than Jace and I. Yet Charlie heading to college hours away from Brockton simply isn't as heart-wrenching for them. And I haven't confided my anxieties to Zoe or Charlie anyway. They wouldn't understand. Jace is going to the University of Colorado, a ten-minute walk from the apartment I share with my Gran.

Here's the thing. Jace Wilder is, like, a celebrity in Brockton. He's expected to be the starting quarterback on the UC football team – yes, as a freshman – and the whole state is looking to him to turn the team's dismal record around. Now, if Jace was boring or shy or just – not Jace – he might not attract quite as much attention. But he's not only a leader on the football team; he's always been the kind of guy other guys – and girls, too – look up to. People want his attention and his approval. I can't explain it. But I want it too.

Then there's his physical appearance. Even if that boy had the personality of a rock and the athleticism of – I don't know, a worm? – even then, heads would turn.

There's no question that the comfortable relationship we've settled into is going to be jostled big time when Jace goes to college. If I thought going from friends to boyfriend-girlfriend was a big change, well, it was somehow way less significant than what we're now facing.

Rolling back my shoulders and stretching my legs, I stand up to jog back to the campsite. My stomach growls in hopes that breakfast will already be cooking by the time I get there. It's still early, but odds are that Jace and Wes are awake. Wesley Jamison is Jace's half-brother – they share a father – but hardly anyone knows this secret family relation. The three of us have been camping with their dad since we were five years old. I learned early on that sleeping in was not an option when camping.

My legs are wobbly when I finally get to the dirt road leading to the campsite. Cars line the road for a quarter mile. The camping trip was meant to be an intimate gathering with a few friends, but it takes a lot of effort to keep any social affair small when Jace Wilder is involved. He doesn't actually invite people himself. He doesn't have to. How word spreads so fast about where he'll be on any particular night is beyond me. But I've come to expect it. And it doesn't bother me like it used to. Jace has proven that when it comes to him and me, the crowds don't really matter.

"Morning, Pepper Jones," a familiar voice greets me.

I turn to see Ryan Harding jogging up behind me, a wide grin spread across his face. He's let his light brown hair grow out a bit, and the tousled strands curl under his ears. As the top male high school distance runner in the country, Ryan's confident and easy stride indicates he's more than ready to take on the college running scene this fall.

"I thought I might see you out this morning," he comments as he syncs his pace with mine.

"Nothing like a sunrise run in the mountains, you know?" He loves to run almost as much as I do.

"It's the best. I went a little longer than I planned and I'm starved now. Is that bacon I smell?"

"It better be. I was dreaming of it the whole way down from DuncanPeak."

"You ran all the way up there?" Ryan asks, startled. "That's, like, a two thousand foot elevation gain, Pepper! You must have been out for hours."

I glance at my watch. "Yeah, coming up on two hours here."

"Coach Tom increased your mileage this summer?" Ryan asks.

"Nah, I went rogue this morning. I mean, I generally follow the training plan, but sometimes I just get carried away and need to keep running, you know?"

"I know, but don't get too carried away, you know my spiel on that," the ever-practical Ryan warns me. He's a big believer that too many high school runners over-train and burn out, or get injuries that ruin their future running careers. He might be right, but I know that most of the top high school runners are putting in way more mileage than Coach Tom currently has me doing. And it makes me nervous. Sure, I won Nationals last year by following his plan, but it seems only logical that I need to train more if I expect to keep improving, or win Nationals again.

Just because Ryan's dad, Mark Harding, is head coach of the UC cross country teams, doesn't mean *Ryan* knows everything about how to train properly.

We slow to a walk as we make our way toward the campfire. Tents are pitched throughout the woods, but the only sound is a low murmuring of voices. At seven AM, most people are still asleep. I could hear them partying from the tent I shared with Jace well into the early morning hours.

I smile when I see Jace standing over a Coleman stove wearing a winter hat and hoodie. The sharp edges of his handsome face contrast with the soft smile he flashes me when he glances up from the stove. His eyes roam over my running clothes before darting to Ryan. His jaw tightens and he returns his attention to the stove.

Ryan and Jace have a complicated relationship. I suppose they call each other friends. They shared the same circle of buddies at Brockton Public, but there's a tension between them that may never dissipate. Ryan was my first boyfriend, and Jace isn't happy that Ryan beat him to it. Jace knows it's his own fault, and there's not much you can hold against a guy like Ryan. Anyway, Ryan isn't much of a jealous guy, but he knows I broke up with him because of my feelings for Jace. So yeah, the awkwardness is hard to avoid.

I wrap my arms around Jace, and feel relieved when he turns around to face me, and pulls me close. He kisses me chastely on the lips and murmurs in my ear, "Don't tell me I missed snuggling with you this morning so you could go for a run with Ryan." His voice is light, but I sense the hurt beneath it.

"I just caught up with him a minute ago, Jace. Now, I'm starving. What'd you make me?" I peek over his shoulder at the skillet.

"Oh, you think these eggs are for you, do you?"

"Not a chance, Pep," Wes's voice booms as he hip-checks me away from Jace and the warm, gooey scrambled eggs. He grins at me, a forkful of eggs already in his mouth.

"Hey buddy, you didn't just run up a mountain. What kind of a friend are you, anyway?" I tease Wes, hands on hips.

"A hungover one. Now, where's that delicious-smelling bacon that got me out of my sleeping bag at this obscene hour?"

Jace hands me a plate of bacon. "You can have Pepper's leftovers, man."

Wes shrugs before shoving another bite of eggs in his mouth.

"I want cheese on my eggs anyway," I say sweetly as I pick up a piece of bacon.

"Well shit, if I knew cheese was an option..." Wes frowns in disappointment at his plain eggs. Jace chuckles beside me.

Ryan has disappeared, and only a few others are up, warming themselves by the campfire and sipping mugs of what I assume is coffee.

Jace pulls me onto his lap in a camp chair, telling me he'll make me cheesy eggs in a minute, and grabbing a piece of bacon for himself. Sighing in contentment, I curl my exhausted body into him and rest my head on his chest. It's safe here, in Jace's arms. Sometimes I can forget it's all about to change.

Wes is puttering around trying to make coffee, and asking Jace every other minute where to find something. Who knew making coffee was so complicated? Wes is a piece of work. He treats partying like I treat running. He loves it with a passion, and is always seeking a better, bigger time. The boy was always a social butterfly growing up, but it seems to have evolved into something else entirely during his high school years. It's like he's chasing after this blissful state he finds with girls and inebriation, or just the high from being surrounded by people. People who adore and worship him – almost like they do Jace. Wes is an enigma to me. Partying definitely doesn't give me a sense of peace and happiness, and I find it hard to believe that's what he gets from it.

Wes seems to have it made – wealthy, athletic, good looking, and smart. He's headed to his dad's alma mater, Princeton, in a week, where he'll play football. So I can't figure out what he's running from.

A girl I've never seen before emerges from Wes's tent, her long dark hair wrapped up in a bun on top of her head. Despite the cold morning air, she wears only a thin camisole and flannel pajama bottoms, which rest low on her hips, displaying her jutting hip bones. A sleeping bag is wrapped around her shoulders like a blanket and she approaches Wesley with a pout.

"Baby, why didn't you wake me up?" she whines while climbing up his body to whisper something in his ear.

Jace isn't paying attention. "I wanted to go on a hike with you today, but you were running for so long, will you be up for it?"

"Of course," I assure him. "That's why I wanted to get my run in early, so we could get going on the hike."

"You can't take a day off from running even if you go on a long hike? If we're going to make it to the waterfall, it's ten miles round trip."

"Nope, I'll get behind on my mileage if I take a day off," I tell him. "Long-distance runners are way more hard core than quarterbacks," I tease.

"You think so, huh?" Jace tickles me until I squirm. I try to suppress my giggles so that I don't wake everyone up, but Jace is relentless and bursts of giggles inevitably erupt. When he finally backs down, I find Wes watching us before crawling into his tent, an unfathomable expression on his face. Before I can decipher the look, the girl's arm pulls him inside, and he zips up the flap.

Jace shuts down various invites to join others on activities, and we successfully manage to go on a hike with just the two of us. It's rare to get Jace alone like this, and I savor the hours of comfortable silence beside him on the trail. Jace sets a brutal pace, and I imagine that's the only reason we were able to dissuade others from joining us on the hike. By the time we hop in his Jeep to head back to Brockton, I'm beyond exhausted.

I must have fallen asleep because I wake to Jace kissing me gently on the forehead. The Jeep is parked outside my apartment building on Shadow Lane, and it's dark outside.

Jace is leaning over to my side, and he cups my chin in his hand. "Hey, sleepy girl."

"Hey," I say softly. I've managed to avoid thinking about it all day, but suddenly the weight of what is about to happen hits me with a force so strong, I can barely hold back the tears threatening to spill. Jace is moving into his dorm tomorrow for football preseason. He won't live down the street anymore.

Jace tucks a loose strand of hair behind my ear. "I texted Buns, she's expecting you for dinner."

"But not you?" I ask, confused. Jace always joins my Gran and me for dinner when he can. He lives with his dad, Jim, and while the two of them have breakfast down pat, their skills at cooking dinner are fairly pathetic. But that's not the only reason Jace is always at our place. He's family. He has his own spot at the table and it feels empty when he's not there. My Gran, Bunny (Buns to Jace), has been helping take care of Jace since he was in diapers.

Jace shakes his head. "Dad wanted to take me and Wes out for dinner one last time before Wes leaves for Princeton." And you for college, I think. Sure, he won't be far, but he'll eat dinner with his team at a special cafeteria for athletes every night instead of with me and Gran.

"Why does this feel like goodbye?" I ask to myself, realizing too late I've said it out loud. "Not to you," I amend, "but to a chapter of our lives?"

"The chapter of Pepper and Jace on Shadow Lane?" Jace asks with a smile.

"Is it silly for me to be so sentimental about this?" I ask him, hoping he'll tell me he feels sad too.

"You've been worried about me starting college all summer, Pep. But things aren't going to change so much. You'll see," Jace tells me. He's so confident, I almost believe him. But I catch the fear lingering in his green eyes.

I kiss him then, hard, hoping to solidify with my lips the faith I have in us. That we will continue to be *us* even as Jace leaves behind his life on Shadow Lane.

Chapter 2

A strange melancholy settles over me when I finally climb out of Jace's Jeep. It follows me through dinner and into bed that night. When I wake up in the morning, a sense of loss is still draped over me like a heavy jacket. I'd take it off if I could, but I know it's no use.

My phone shows several missed texts and phone calls. Zoe dropped Charlie off at Mountain West yesterday and wants to go on a run with me today. Jace returned from dinner with his dad and brother late last night, and apparently stayed up most of the night packing. I have one voicemail I must have received while hiking yesterday that I never checked before going to sleep.

I hold my breath as I hear the University of Oregon's head coach introduce herself. Wow. The head coach from the reigning Division I National Champions. Most of the calls up until now were from assistant coaches. I've been hoping to get invited for a recruitment trip to Oregon, if only because my running idol, Elsa Blackwood, went there. After college, Elsa turned to marathons, and, now in her thirties, she's still the best female American distance runner. Hands down.

There's no way I'll actually go to Oregon for college though. My life is here, in Brockton, and I doubt I'll ever leave. But I'm still flattered the coach called me, and I'm not against visiting the school for kicks.

I know I should wait to run with Zoe, who surely wants to recap the goodbye with Charlie, but I need to be alone this morning. Zoe likes to chat away her emotions; I like to run mine away. Seriously, running somehow makes things better. Not all the way better, but enough.

My loyal mutt, Dave, pants quietly beside me as we wind our way through the neighborhood and onto my favorite trail up the foothills. My legs are sore from the run and hike yesterday, and it takes a while before they loosen up. I've trained harder this summer than ever before. After winning Nationals last fall, I felt overwhelmed by the pressure during track season. Instead of embracing the challenge of living up to my title as the best female high school distance runner in the country, I completely shied away from it. I feared racing, and found myself more excited about my newfound social life as Jace's girlfriend than I was about racing.

Somehow, by facing my fears in my relationship with Jace head on – which entailed confronting the ultimate mean girl, Madeline Brescoll, about trying to sabotage our relationship – I also gained the confidence to face my fears on the track.

I know that if I want to be the National Champion again, I can't coast my way through the summer. Normally, my summer training entails running five to six days a week, with at least one day off from working out each week. With the exception of one long run a week, the rest of the runs Coach Tom has me doing are at an easy pace and no more than five or six miles. I haven't talked much with Coach this summer, probably because he figures I'm just doing the same base mileage routine I did last year. But I'm not. I've nearly doubled my weekly mileage, and I never take a day off. I also lift weights every other day. When I show up for our first practice, I'll be in the best shape of my life.

Ryan and Coach Tom both drilled into my head the importance of pacing myself – not just in a race, but in training over the course of a season. I get it, but I've never been injured before. I've never really tested myself. I've never trained so hard I thought I might break. Sure, I've raced like that, and occasionally I'll have brutal workouts, but Coach always makes sure I get plenty of rest. Since I've started talking to college coaches, I've heard plenty about other high school training programs. Most college coaches are surprised, if not shocked, when they hear how low my weekly mileage has been with Coach Tom. If I don't step it up on my own, I'll never be ready for college training.

When Dave and I turn back onto Shadow Lane, I find myself running up to the Wilders' house instead of our apartment building. Running worked its magic. The veil of melancholy has dissipated to a dull ache that I've grown used to suppressing.

Jim waves hello to me from the breakfast table and Dave meanders to the kitchen, hunting for scraps, while I make my way down the stairs of their bi-level house. I'm not surprised Jace is still asleep. He has the entire downstairs to himself, and I wonder if Jim will change the space when Jace moves out.

Jace's lower body is tangled in his bed sheets, and I drink in the sight of his broad back before jumping on the bed next to him. Expecting to startle him awake, he takes me by surprise, tackling me onto my back and smothering me with kisses.

"I heard you coming down the stairs," he tells me between kisses. "You think you're pretty stealth, but I was just lying in wait."

My giggling dies down when I take in the boxes stacked up at the end of his bed. I went straight for Jace, and didn't notice how empty the rest of his room was.

Jace follows my gaze. "I hope you came ready to work," he tells me.

"You want me to help you move?" I ask. We have avoided talking about the move. Avoided talking about college. But it's here now, and it can't be ignored any longer.

Jace turns to look at me. "I assumed you would." His voice holds a question.

What exactly are you asking me, Jace? Do you want me to stay by your side? Or do you want some space? Are you going to put distance between us in more ways than one?

"I will," I assure him.

I watch Jace dig through what's left in his closet for a pair of athletic shorts.

"Hey, I almost forgot!" I tell him. "The head coach from Oregon called and invited me on a recruit trip."

Jace pauses before pulling on his shorts slowly. "You sound really excited." His voice is flat, his jaw tense.

"Well, yeah. It's Oregon. The best running program in the country. Elsa Blackwood went there."

"The marathoner?"

"Yeah."

"Are you going?" Jace asks, unmoving.

"On the recruit trip? Yeah, I mean, it's a free trip. But I'm going to UC, Jace. You know that's never been a question."

Jace shrugs. "If you go visit other schools, you might change your mind."

"You didn't," I remind him.

Jace runs a hand over his face. "I know," he admits. "We need breakfast," he announces, steering the conversation away from dangerous territory. Talk about the future must be avoided at all costs. It's simply too scary. The unknown.

***

Jace is in a dorm reserved for freshman and sophomore athletes. I don't know what makes these dorms special – I suppose less partying so the athletes can sleep. But I do know that Jace's dorm is guys-only. Most of the other freshmen are housed in co-ed dorms and I'm thankful other girls won't be ogling him as he walks down the hall from the showers in a towel. I'll be the first to admit how powerful that image is, and I don't want anyone else getting its effect but me.

Jim pulls his pickup into a crowded lot and we start to unload the truck bed. Before we can make the first trip up to the third floor, three guys approach the pickup.

"Hi there, we're here to help you move in," the one with Greek lettering on his shirt announces, as he looks us over. "You must be Jace Wilder," he says with a politician's smile. He reaches out his hand to shake Jace's. "Gage Fitzgerald, president of Sig Beta, and these are two of our pledges." He gestures to an

14

absurdly tall guy with a buzz cut, and a nervous kid who doesn't look old enough to be a college student.

Gage doesn't offer the pledges' names but moves along, introducing himself to Jim and me. He seems to know who we are already and it unnerves me.

The pledges unload boxes and duffel bags from the truck's bed, and Jim, Jace and I ignore Gage's protests and fill our arms. I can hear him rambling on about various upcoming social events as we make our way up the staircase and I'm happy to hear Jim tell the fraternity guys we can take it from here. It's a relief when it's just the three of us in the dorm room. I need to process this. Take it all in without any distractions. This is Jace's new life.

The room is too warm and I crack a window before plopping down on Jace's rolled-up comforter in the middle of the room. It's a common area with four bedroom doors in addition to the main door to the hallway. Someone else has already started moving in because a mini fridge is hooked into an outlet and one of the bedroom doors is propped open with a fan.

We're all silent, breathing heavily from hauling everything up the stairs, as we look around. Jace pulls the key he was given from his back pocket and unlocks the door with the letter B on it. Before he has a chance to look inside, a bellowing voice greets us. "Hey! The first roommate has arrived," he greets us jovially. I swivel around to find a very large bald man filling the main entry. Not exactly fat, just extremely . . . big. Meaty is the word that pops into my mind. A meaty bald man. "Frankie!" he hollers over his shoulder.

A younger version of the man peeks his head over his father's shoulder. "Oh, you're right there, Frankie," the older ones says. "Your first roommate is here."

Frankie might be younger but if possible, he is even larger than his father. Frankie's face breaks into a grino when he sees Jace. Jim and I exchange confused glances when Jace and Frankie head toward each other for a manly hug.

"You're my roommate? I seriously have to put up with your stink for an entire year?" Jace jokes, punching Frankie's humongous bicep.

Frankie rubs his arm in fake pain. "Dude, you know I'm your dream roommate." Frankie finally looks around, noticing his audience for the first time. When his eyes lock on me, his smile gets even wider.

"You must be Miss Pepper," Frankie says as he makes his way toward me. "I'm Franklin Zimmer."

When I stand up, I'm enveloped in a bear hug. "It's nice to meet you," I manage to get out, though it's muffled.

"All right, all right, take it easy, Frankie," Jace mock-warns.

As the introductions are made, we learn that Frankie and Jace were roommates for two summers at football camp in Texas. Once that's been established, I recall Jace mentioning Frankie on several occasions, especially when he found out Frankie would be a freshman with him at UC.

Frankie's from Kansas, and his dad, Rick, is disappointed Frankie isn't going to his alma mater, KU. Frankie tells us not to feel sorry for Rick because he has four more opportunities to see a son play football at KU, since Frankie has four younger brothers.

The afternoon is spent unpacking and the sick feeling in the pit of my stomach grows as the boxes and bags empty out.

"All right man, we gotta head out for practice in five!" Frankie calls from his bedroom several hours later.

Jim says a quick goodbye to Jace. They aren't sentimental types. And besides, he's not going to be far away. Geographically, that is. Frankie and Rick have been going on about all the various football workouts and social functions lined up for the team over the next few weeks, and I know I won't be seeing much of Jace.

It's just me and Jace in the room now, and he tugs the bottom of my tee shirt until I'm close to him. There's no denying how I feel any more. The fear is weighing down on me, making it hard to breathe.

"Pep." Jace's voice is pained, and I know he can read the emotions on my face. "It's going to be okay, you know? Of course it will be different, but we'll be fine."

"Yeah, I know." The confidence in my voice is false, and we both know it. "I just hate change," I finally admit after a moment of silence. And upon that admission, a stupid tear escapes and trickles down the side of my face. I quickly wipe it with the back of my hand and look away. "Argh!" I feel like stomping my foot in frustration, hating myself for acting like such an emotional girl.

This is Jace Wilder, and you don't ease into anything with him. We won't ease into this transition. It will come on full force, like everything does with Jace. And when it hits us we won't be the same. Maybe it will be a good change, and maybe it won't.

When Frankie returns, our goodbye is cut short with a brief kiss before Jace is hustling me down to the pickup so he can head over to the field house.

Zoe's sitting on the stairs outside my apartment building when Jim drops me off a few minutes later, and I'm thankful for the distraction. She gives me an annoyed look for blowing her off this morning, but all it takes is a simple apology from me, explaining it was Jace's moving day, and she's over it.

Instead of hearing all about her trip to Mountain West yesterday, Zoe surprises me with news of a party she is dragging me to later tonight. Normally I would beg off immediately – I'm usually only one for big parties if Jace is with me – but I'm reluctant to be alone with my thoughts tonight. Gran has bridge night and the apartment holds too much of Jace – too much of him that is already starting to feel like the past. Like distant nostalgic memories.

"Yeah, so I ran into Dana this morning at the gas station and Tina's throwing this end-of-the-summer thing. I guess we hadn't heard about it because it's not, like, something everyone at Public is invited to," Zoe explains. As usual, she's practically bouncing with energy. "I got the feeling it was sort of exclusive, and that Dana thought she was doing me a big favor inviting us. And she made sure to tell me at least three times that you should come too."

I roll my eyes as I fill two glasses with lemonade from the fridge, handing one to Zoe. "Cheers." We clink glasses.

"To senior year!" Zoe raises her glass.

Senior year. Why do I not share Zoe's excitement?

Zoe continues, "I mean, I know Dana and Tina think they're better than everyone, but I figure it *is* our senior year after all, and we should try to have fun, right? So we are totally going to this party. If it's lame, we can leave."

Dana Foster and Tina Anderson have been the popular girls in our grade since middle school. They tried to befriend me when I was in eighth grade and essentially friendless since Jace and Wes left for high school. It wasn't hard to ascertain that they were using me to get to Jace and Wes. That they thought I was only worthy of being their friend because of my friendship with two of the most popular guys in Brockton. Some things never change, apparently.

I don't doubt that Zoe sees through Tina and Dana too; she's not stupid. But she doesn't care. Zoe doesn't let much bother her.

We hadn't been part of the parties or associated with the popular people for most of high school, and we were comfortable on the sidelines. Our running teammates were our friends, and that was all we needed. But then Ryan Harding came to town our junior year, and his instant popularity offered a bridge between the running crowd and the partying scene. And then Jace Wilder became my boyfriend, and, well, going to parties became a regular part of our lives.

"Fine, just let me shower and get something to eat," I appease her.

"Excellent!" she says with a little clap. "Rollie and Omar are picking us up in twenty, so be quick."

I raise my eyebrows at her presumptive planning before heading to the bathroom. With Charlie Owens and Claire Padilla graduated, Roland Fowler and Omar Hernandez are the only teammates left we are close friends with. I've become closer with Jenny Mendoza, another teammate, since she started working at the same restaurant as me this summer, but she's only a sophomore.

Rollie's a nerd at heart, but he's transformed into sort of a cool nerd since joining the partying scene with us last year. Omar has always been the most socially accepted amongst our running friends because he plays varsity baseball in the spring. I'm not surprised he got an invite to Tina's party, and with Rollie as his best friend, they sort of come as a package. Like Zoe and me. You don't invite one without the other.

In some ways, with Jace off at college, things have returned to the status quo. Zoe and I will spend more time together with our boyfriends gone, and the main focus in my life will return to running. I let the warm water run over my sticky skin and shake my head at this foolish thought. Ever since Jace became more than a friend, I knew my life would never be the same.

Chapter 3

The party at Tina's *is* lame, but apparently my friends don't share my opinion. There are about two dozen people at her house, all congregated in the open kitchen and living room area. It's classier than any party I've been to, and I'm glad I'm wearing a sundress instead of my usual cutoff shorts and plain cotton tee shirt. People are drinking wine in actual wine glasses, and there are little cheese cubes with toothpicks and an assortment of healthy cracker options laid out on the counter.

Not that I've ever been a big drinker, but I stopped drinking any alcohol at the beginning of the summer when I ramped up my training. I need to eliminate any potential weaknesses this cross season and drinking and National Champion don't seem to go together. I'm probably the only one in the room drinking water, and my annoyance that I promised to be the DD tonight isn't because I feel like drinking. It's because I'd rather go home and get a good night's sleep before weight lifting tomorrow morning. School starts in a couple days, and I need to maintain a decent sleep routine if I expect to lift weights at the gym before classes three times a week.

Zoe is basking in a newfound popularity, which I find amusing given her past criticisms of the very girls she now chats with happily. It doesn't bother me though. Not really. Maybe she needs a distraction from Charlie leaving, and I can't blame her for that.

Rollie actually seems to have the attention of not one, but two girls, who I recognize as juniors on the soccer team. But what shocks me the most is Omar, who is practically groping Tina on the couch. Tina Anderson. The classic social-climber. I thought Omar had better taste than that. But I'm here too, at her house, so who am I to judge?

I didn't think I'd miss the Barbies – Zoe's label for the three most popular girls at Brockton Public last year, who have since graduated. They could be petty and social-climbing but they were a lot more down to earth than the girls I've talked to tonight.

I've texted Jace already, who is at a team meeting, and has an early morning workout tomorrow. I make my way outside to the porch, and I discover it wraps around the entire house. Finding a comfortable porch chair by the front door, I settle in and, without thinking, I find Wes's number on my contacts and tap his name.

"Pep, what's going on?" he answers on the first ring.

I tell him where I am, and he immediately senses that I'm not exactly having the time of my life.

"Want me to pick you up?" he asks.

"Nah, I'm the DD so I need to stick around," I explain. "I just felt like talking, and Jace is at a team meeting."

"Oh yeah, right." The tinge of hurt in his voice makes me realize I've just told him he's my second choice, and I cringe. But what's the big deal, obviously my boyfriend is my first choice, right?

"What are you up to?" I wonder, surprised to realize there's no background noise or indication he's out with others.

"Just home, watching TV."

It's silent for a moment as I process Wes's tone. He sounds down, and I can't even remember the last time Wesley Jamison sounded bummed out.

"Hmmm..." I drawl out, hoping to get Wes talking.

"I'm not going to Princeton next week," Wes finally says on a long breath.

"What?" I couldn't have heard that right.

"Princeton. I'm not going. I'm deferring a year."

"What?" I ask again. "Why? When did you decide this?" I've always had this feeling Wes was going to mess up his life somehow with all the partying he does. It's been on the verge of out-of-control pretty much since we rekindled our friendship about a year ago. And I'm afraid my fear is now true.

"I guess I've been thinking about it for a while but I just told my dad like, a couple hours ago. David, that is. I haven't told Jim yet." David is the one everyone else thinks is Wes's father. The one he's called Dad his whole life. Jim is Wes's real biological father. And Jace's too. "I haven't told anyone else yet, actually. I wanted to make this decision on my own. And David was the hardest one to tell. Jim, Jace, my mom, they won't flip their shit like he did."

"Yeah? What'd he do?"

And that question is all it takes. The floodgates open and Wes tells me just how screwed up his relationship with his non-biological father is. David had always known that Wes was the product of his wife's affair. In some ways, David acted like it didn't bother him. That was most likely because David himself has had countless affairs. "He probably has other kids out there somewhere. It wouldn't surprise me if I had more half-siblings I don't even know about," Wes says bitterly.

"What's fucked up is that I'm like a toy or something to him. He's hardly ever around, but he's always controlling me with his demands, his money, and my mom. He knows we depend on him and we need him. My mom should've just divorced him years ago but she's afraid she won't get much. Apparently there was a prenup, but I don't know much about it."

I've always known things weren't exactly all warm and fuzzy in the Jamison household, but I'd never witnessed the anger Wes held toward David. "He uses me to brag to his friends about, to give himself credibility as a good guy who can raise a good kid, but David didn't do a damn thing to raise me besides write a few checks. Big ones, but they sure as hell didn't come with a fatherly hug. I only get those if his business buddies are around."

David's a hot shot movie producer and he's usually out of town, traveling to LA or exotic settings. I don't know much about it and I don't really care. He's just this intimidating unseen presence at the Jamison mansion. I've known Wesley most of my life and can count on one hand the number of times I've met David.

"Anyway, he's always made it clear I'm going to Princeton. And it's not like it's a shitty college," Wes says with a dark chuckle, "so who am I to complain? But I can't do it, Pep, not now. I don't know what I want to study or do with my life. I don't know if I want to throw myself into football or not. If I'm on the team, that's it. That's my college life. Football. And that's cool for Jace but I don't know if I want that. I've lived a pretty fucking sheltered life." Wes's voice is bitter, and I sense a lot of it is directed at himself. "I'm a spoiled brat, Pep, and I don't want to spend college wasting it all away."

The self-hatred underlying that statement stabs at my gut, and I hunch over in pain for Wes. I want to tell myself he's just in a bad mood, a "funk". He's worried about going off to some prestigious college, worried he's not worthy of it. But I know it runs deeper than that.

"Wes, most college freshmen have no idea what they want to do with their lives. And a lot of people who graduate college, too. Plenty of people waste their college years. That doesn't make you a spoiled brat, or a loser, or whatever you are telling yourself." My words feel empty, but I have to say them anyway. "What are you planning on doing now?" I ask, when I realize he's not going to respond to my comments.

"I'm gonna work. I've never actually earned any money before, can you believe that?" His dark laugh is haunting. "David made me do internships and shit, but I've never had a real job. And maybe I just want a simple life. Maybe I don't want to accomplish something amazing or be someone my dad can brag about. Is that so bad?" Wes wants me to answer, but his thoughts are all over the place and I'm having trouble keeping up.

"No, that's not bad," I say slowly, wondering what exactly we're talking about.

"Jim and Bunny are happier than any adults I've met in my parents' world and they live simply. Why does everything have to be on a grand scale? Big house, fancy cars, you know?" Wes's voice is speeding up and I'm starting to wonder if he's on something. Unfortunately, I've witnessed enough to know the signs of drug use, and I know Wes sometimes uses them recreationally at parties. Nothing serious, and not often, as far as I know. But he's home alone and he's not himself. I'm worried.

"Look Wes, why don't I come over and hang out for a bit with you? We can talk about all this." I try to sound cool, like it's no big deal, but my mind is racing. My primary thought is that he shouldn't be alone. Even if he's totally sober, I've never heard him so worked up, and it's making me uneasy. I can't ask Jace to go. He just started preseason and he can't afford to lose sleep his first night. Wes's friends from Lincoln Academy – the private high school he graduated from – have already left for college. I don't have Pierce's or Forbes's phone numbers anyway. So I'm the one who needs to be there. That's that.

Wes, Jace and I were inseparable until they started high school. Jace and Wes had a falling out, which I've since learned was tied to their discovering they were brothers. It never made perfect sense to me, as learning my best friend was my sibling would only make me closer to that person, but I've accepted it. Over the past year, the three of us have become friends again, and we've spent a lot of time together the past few months. Things changed but they didn't. He might be my boyfriend's secret half-brother, but he's still like family to me.

I head inside to find my friends. Zoe appears deep in conversation with Dana, who is swaying back and forth clutching a glass of red wine and nodding her head solemnly.

"Zoe, I need to head out now," I interrupt her, recognizing that waiting patiently will get me nowhere. "I can give you a ride home now or pick you up later tonight."

"Oh, you aren't staying here?" Dana asks.

"No, I have to head out," I tell her.

"The Andersons are in Barbados and Tina's aunt is supposed to be watching her, but she's at her boyfriend's place tonight so everyone can totally crash here," Dana explains.

"I'll just stay here," Zoe says with a shrug. "My parents think I'm at your house tonight anyway." Zoe has really improved her lying abilities over the past year. Mr. Burton is notoriously strict and would ground her for life if he knew what she was up to. He's a cop and seems to know all the goings-on, so I'm surprised she can get away with being out all night. I suppose having four younger siblings provides a decent distraction.

Rollie and Omar are similarly uninterested in leaving and Rollie sends me off with his car keys, not even asking what time I'll pick him up tomorrow morning. I'll probably be awake well before they are, so as long as I can drop the car and jog to the gym for my lifting routine, I'm not worried. Rollie's recently traded out his glasses for contacts and given that the two soccer girls are still staring at him in rapt attention, I'd say the new look is working for him.

When I pull up to the Jamison's mansion a few minutes later, the house is dark and it looks like no one is awake. I'm about to text Wes to confirm he's still home and that I won't be waking his parents, when the front door swings open.

Wes looks happy to see me, but an absence of the usual brightness and energy behind his smile is evident.

He leads me to his downstairs den, where we've spent many hours over the years watching movies. Come to think of it, Jace and his brother are both a bit subterranean, given how much time they spend in

27

basements. A baseball game is on, and a bowl of popcorn sits on the coffee table. I glance around suspiciously, looking for signs of drinking or anything else odd. I find none.

I peer at Wes, who is watching me expectantly, and though his eyes look both exhausted and frenzied, they are clear. "You okay?" I ask, genuinely curious how he will answer.

"Not really. It's like everything I've been ignoring that's shitty about my life has hit me, and I knew I couldn't go to Princeton next week. And now that I told my dad I'm relieved but, like, kind of fucked in the head too."

We sit on the couch facing each other, and I just listen. Wes talks for hours about his screwed-up family, his unknown future, his desire for something sure and real in his life. Jace, Jim, me, that's all he really has. He loves his mom but she's "a hot mess". It really begins to dawn on me how alone he is. His parents are never here and this giant house feels empty.

Wes is so different from his brother. Jace never opens up like this. Jace will talk to me more than anyone but usually it takes prodding, and it's rarely more than a short statement. Jace doesn't get into the layers behind his emotions, the complexities of what makes him who he is. And it's not like Jace doesn't have complicated emotional layers to sort out. His mother leaving him at a young age definitely messed with his head, but he won't say so. Now that she's back and is recovering from addiction, Jace still doesn't open up much about his feelings on the situation.

Eventually Wes tires of talking. He seems to feel better after letting it all out, and I try to listen to everything he has to say, knowing it's special he's chosen me to say it to. Sometimes girls are just easier to talk to about emotional stuff, and he may never have a discussion like this with Jace or Jim. Wes pulls an old worn box down from a shelf, and I recognize the Noah's Ark jigsaw puzzle. It's been years since I've done a puzzle with Wes. The three of us used to stay up late as kids trying to finish puzzles together, and I remember this one took us nearly an entire summer to complete. Jace and I still do puzzles together sometimes, but Wes usually can't sit still long enough to do one anymore.

Wes keeps asking if it's okay I'm still at his house, and I reassure him I texted Gran that I was here. I think he's asking more about Jace, but honestly I bet Jace will be happy I was here for Wes. I didn't text Jace where I was going because I didn't want him worrying about Wes all night.

Now that I know Wes is okay, or at least, he will be, my biggest concern is actually my training. I can't miss a day of weight training because it will screw up my whole schedule. I could try to catch up on sleep after my workout but I have a shift at the Tavern.

We've been working on the puzzle for over an hour and barely gotten the edge pieces sorted when I decide I better call it a night. It's nearly three in the morning. Wes walks me to my car and holds me in a hug before sending me home. I know he's thankful I'm here for him, and that he shared a lot of intimate details about his life, but I feel like he may have held on just a little too tightly. I hope he doesn't need more from me than I can give.

Chapter 4

Zoe, Omar, and Rollie are remarkably unfazed that I spent most of the night at Wes's place. I leave the explanation vague, and they don't pry. Over the past year, my friends' curiosity about Wesley Jamison hasn't necessarily dwindled, but they've come to accept that Wes's place in my life is a unique one that they may never understand.

As the sun rises, Rollie drops me off at the UC gym before heading home – presumably to go straight to sleep. The three of them look like they've been up all night. But the party hadn't held the allure those kinds of gatherings used to hold for me. Without Jace Wilder there, I simply didn't have the desire to rally the energy for it.

The gym has only just opened and the kid behind the check-in counter doesn't look much more awake than my friends had. He glances at my temporary gym pass and nods groggily before returning his focus to the computer screen and Starbucks cup in front of him. UC gives access to its facilities to Brockton Public varsity athletes at certain times when it's not as busy. At six in the morning, the weight machines are completely empty.

The peppy beat of hip hop is the only sound in the otherwise silent space. I've just completed the first set of my routine when I notice a guy standing in front of a wall of mirrors lifting weights. He's tall – as tall as Jace, who is six feet three inches – and his broad shoulders and narrow hips signal he's an athlete, and probably not a high school one. He's wearing a baseball cap that shadows his face but I'm able to decipher enough of his features in the mirror to recognize him. Clayton Dennison.

I quickly turn away, heading to the water fountain to grab a drink before starting my next set. I doubt Clayton remembers me. He was a senior at Brockton Public when I was a freshman. In a way, he was the Jace Wilder of his class, though never quite as ... well... he wasn't Jace. And Clayton knew it.

Clayton was captain of the baseball team and he wasn't pleased when Jace came in as a freshman and threatened his spot as starting pitcher. I was still in junior high, but I heard Jace slept with Clayton's ex-girlfriend only a week after they broke up. Eventually, Clayton must have realized it was better to be Jace's friend than his enemy, and he apparently got over their differences. It probably didn't hurt that Jace announced his intent to focus on football as his primary sport, and, though he became the lead pitcher after Clayton graduated, Jace took a step back from his baseball ambitions and didn't challenge Clayton's spot. Which worked out for Clayton, who is – along with Ryan Harding and Jace Wilder, of course – one of Brockton's most decorated athletes.

Settling into the leg press machine, I sigh, realizing I fall into that exclusive group as well. Brockton's a unique place. At nearly 6,000 feet altitude at the base of the foothills and not far from the Rocky Mountains, Brockton is full of athletic people. The Olympic Training Center isn't far away and a number of professional athletes train in Brockton. I've lived here my whole life, so I forget that most people don't work out every day. That sports aren't at the center of everyone's world. Here in Brockton, we love our sports. And our athletes.

Local pride is a big deal, and when Clayton Dennison signed with UC at Brockton, people went crazy. Just like they did when Jace signed last year. Ryan Harding got attention too, but runners just don't have the fan base football and baseball get. Personally, I prefer to stay under the radar as much as possible.

But I don't always get what I want.

"Pepper Jones?" Clayton Dennison is standing in front of me. I glance his way as I push the weight on my legs forward with an un-ladylike growl. I increased the weight this morning and boy am I feeling the burn.

I slowly lower the weight to resting before replying, "Hi, Clayton."

"I never see anyone here before seven this time of year. You're hardcore, huh?"

I shrug. "Not any more than you are."

We chat idly about training for a few minutes. I can feel him checking me out, sizing me up. It's awkward. Clayton tried asking me to prom – his senior prom – when I was a freshman. Though Clayton and Jace played nice and acted like they were friends, I saw through it. They hung out with the same people, the popular crowd of course, but it didn't take a genius to figure out Clayton had asked me to prom to piss off Jace, whom he still undoubtedly felt threatened by. As a sophomore, Jace was already stealing Clayton's limelight, which I'm sure he was planning on basking in his senior year. Me, I was a nobody. No one had asked me out before. I stuck with my running friends and secretly crushed on Jace, who only hung out with me outside of school. I'd never thought about other guys because he was it for me.

So I'd said no when Clayton asked me to prom one day after track practice. I didn't even make an excuse. I knew he was using me to get under Jace's skin – even then, everyone knew we were close childhood friends – and I wasn't happy about it.

I still remember Clayton's shocked expression when I turned him down. I turned right around and walked away, but it didn't feel powerful. I was angry and hurt. I never told anyone he asked me, not even Zoe or Gran, and he must have kept the information to himself too. Otherwise, the gossip would have been unbearable. For both of us.

He's being perfectly polite now, though, and that all happened a long time ago. High school is a thing of the past for Clayton.

"So, you and Jace, huh?" he asks. Clayton lifts the brim of his hat and pushes some hair to the side before settling the hat back on his head.

"Oh, yeah. We're together." I'm not sure what exactly he's getting at. Could this be any more awkward?

"Yeah, I ran into Wilder yesterday. It's practically the only thing he wanted to talk to me about, not that I didn't already know. Wilder's dating status is a hot topic with the ladies." Clayton raises his eyebrows knowingly and I roll my eyes in response, pretending his comment doesn't bother me. Which it shouldn't, because it comes as no surprise. "You better watch your back when you come on campus, Ms. Jones." His eyes are smiling at me, but if he knew my history with Jace's female fan club, or one fan in particular, he would realize this is no joking matter.

"I can handle myself," I say, in what I hope is an equally light-hearted tone.

"Well, if you need backup, let me know."

I can't help but frown at him.

"You know," he adds, presumably in response to my confused expression, "the baseball and football teams hang in the same places with the same people. I'm sure we'll be running into each other more." He winks before wandering back to the other side of the room.

The conversation leaves me unsettled for the rest of my workout, despite Clayton's casual demeanor and the easy smile and wave he sends my way when I leave. I don't have a car so I'm preparing to jog the mile and a half home when I turn the corner and nearly run into another familiar Brockton athlete. Ryan Harding is just as startled to see me and I get the impression he was deep in thought.

After my encounter with Clayton, it's a comfort to see Ryan but I'm not sure the feeling is reciprocated. It's unusual to see this distressed expression on Ryan's s

"Oh, hey Pepper." Like me, he's dressed to work out.

"What's up? Everything okay?"

"Yeah, yeah. It's good. Just getting some weights in before meeting up with the team."

"I thought the cross team did all their workouts together? I saw you all in here the other day lifting."

"Oh yeah, we do. I just..." he drifts off, "wanted to burn some energy, you know?"

"Yeah, okay." Something's definitely up with him, because Ryan Harding never deviates from the training plan. He is constantly telling me how important it is not to over-train, and here he is getting in an extra workout before team practice? It's preseason, so they're already training more than they will once classes start.

"You sure you're okay?"

Ryan shifts on his feet and opens his mouth to say something when a loud rowdy group floods out from the athletes' cafeteria across the street and heads in our direction. Another team here for preseason, and, judging by the size of some of them, I'm guessing it's the football team. The field house is just behind the gym and Jace told me they had seven AM practice there.

"Anyway, Pep, I'll check in with you later, cool?" He's already walking away before I can respond. The door to the gym swings open and Ryan nods to Clayton, who is leaving.

Clayton heads my way. "Oh good, you're still here. I was going to see if you needed a ride. Or, you know, I could get you into the cafeteria if you wanted some breakfast."

Okay, now I'm really confused. We aren't friends. We never were. He knows I'm with Jace. He can't seriously still be trying to piss Jace off. Is he that hung up on the competition from his high school glory days? I mean, he's in college now, and is living a whole new level of glory ... ohhhh. It dawns on me. History is repeating itself for Clayton Dennison.

The whole town, and maybe even the entire state, is hyped up for Jace to join the UC football team. Not to mention... *Wilder's dating status is a hot topic with the ladies.* Yup, Clayton is surely aware that Jace Wilder is once again threatening his status as the hottest athlete on campus.

"Dennison." The familiar voice approaching us is dark and dangerous and there is no doubt Jace Wilder knows exactly what Clayton is up to.

Jace places a possessive hand on my hip and he's standing so close behind me, I can feel his chest rising and falling. I don't need to look to know his teammates have paused en route to the field house. Not only has the rowdy group grown quiet, but their presence is heavy and unmistakable. Ryan's in the gym now, thankfully. I might feel comforted and safe in Jace's arms, but I also feel ridiculous. All I wanted was a quiet workout and instead I've caused a scene. A showdown between two high school frenemies. I want to melt into the sidewalk. Anything to escape this embarrassment.

"Jace," I say quietly, trying to convey in my tone that now is not the time or place to hash this out.

Clayton is smiling at him, acting like this is such a lovely coincidence, when we all know it's not. Clayton saw the team coming and he timed his exit from the gym perfectly.

"You guys must have practice," Clayton says, nodding toward the giants looming behind me. "I can make sure your girl here gets home safely, man."

Feeling Jace's hold tighten, I say quickly, "No thanks, I need to jog home anyway as my cool-down." It takes a bit of effort in Jace's stiff grip, but I'm able to turn enough to face my boyfriend, whose green eyes flash dangerously at Clayton. Yikes. I had no idea of the tension between these two.

With an air of nonchalance I kiss Jace lightly on the cheek, whisper quietly enough that hopefully Clayton, but not the entire football team, hears, "I love you." And wave as I jog away, calling, "See you after my shift!" which we hadn't discussed, and I don't know if he's free, but figure I need to break the icy cold air hovering in my wake somehow.

I practically sprint home. Clayton Dennison is the last thing we need right now.

Apparently my boyfriend not only attracts jealous girls – whom I've already learned to deal with – he attracts jealous boys too.

Chapter 5

My shift at the Tavern is from eleven to four and I'd love to take a nap beforehand but instead, I pause outside my apartment building briefly before continuing to jog along the sidewalk toward the bike path. Despite my exhaustion, there's little chance I'll fall asleep, and I want to get my daily run in before my shift so I can see Jace afterward. The jog back from the gym wasn't long enough.

By the time 4:00 rolls around, I'm dead on my feet. The shift was a blur. Gran picks me up and shakes her head at my pathetic state before handing me my cell phone, which I accidentally left at home. The mailbox is full. Missed calls from Zoe, Jace, Wes, Ryan, Rollie, and, surprisingly, Kayla Chambers. Kayla was the most popular girl at Brockton Public last year – the lead Barbie, as Zoe would say – and she ended up having my back. I wouldn't say we're exactly close though, and I certainly didn't expect to be hearing from her once the summer was over. Along with Lisa Delany – Ryan's girlfriend – she will be a freshman at UC this year too. The third girl in their group, Andrea Hill, headed to college out of state.

My friends rarely leave voicemails, but they all have something to tell me today, apparently. I skip through to Jace's message first, planning to listen to the others after, but when I hear his voice asking me to come over after my shift, I forget all about the others and ask Gran to head to the dorms.

I text Jace I'll be there in a minute and he's waiting outside when Gran pulls up. He kisses her on the cheek through the window, and promises to stay out of trouble, giving her his most mischievous grin.

Jace races me up the stairs and into his room without saying hello to his roommates, then shuts the door.

"Damn, it's been the longest fucking twenty-four hours, Pepper." And with that, his mouth is on mine in a frenzied kiss that leaves me breathless. And I'm a long-distance runner, so that's saying something.

Jace tends to take things slowly and cautiously with me. He knows he's got way more experience than me and even after months as his girlfriend, that remains true. His patience puzzled and frustrated me for a while, but I understand it now. It's right between us not to rush or hurry this part of our relationship. If we did, it would consume me completely, I have no doubt about it.

But right now, in this moment, I am surrendering to him because I sense he needs me to, and it feels good. Really good. He's holding me tight, showing me I'm his and I shouldn't ever doubt it. His love for me is in his kiss, and I try to give him all of mine right back.

We're panting when he finally slows his kisses to a brush of my lips, my forehead, and then he slumps on his desk chair, bringing me down with him.

"So, how was your day?" I ask him, giggling.

"Well, it didn't get off to the greatest start," he responds, but it's not with anger. He was heated at the time, and he now appears resigned to dealing with guys like Clayton Dennison. They will probably always be in his life.

"Tell me about practice, your teammates, your other roommates. I want to know everything."

And he does. He delves into the world of Jace Wilder, and I learn the names of his coaches, some weird quirks of his teammates, and, most importantly, that there is a twenty-four-hour ice cream bar at the athletes' cafeteria. "Frankie ate three bowls of mint chocolate chip for breakfast. It was disgusting."

"What else?" I love this, listening to Jace talk. When he lived down the street, I knew so much about his daily life already, he never needed to share like this. But listening to him re-tell it is more enjoyable than I imagined, and I'm beginning to look forward to establishing a routine like this every day.

"My mom came to our afternoon practice," Jace tells me.

I sit up, surprised. "Annie?" Like he has another mom.

"Yeah, it was funny. She was just sitting in the stands when I glanced that way at one point. You know, there are always a bunch of people watching our practices, so it wasn't like she was the only one. I think she feels like she missed out, you know? On going to my practices growing up and stuff. So she's trying to make up for it."

I can tell Jace is touched by this. Really touched. His face softens, and he looks young and vulnerable. Not many people see this side of Jace Wilder. Annie left when Jace was a toddler and she returned last year, sober for the first time in years and seeking to rebuild a relationship with her son. I was distrustful and disdainful of her, but I've started to realize she might be for real. Part of me still fears she will hurt Jace again, and it will be even worse than before she came back, because he has renewed hope. He turns into this little boy when he talks about her. And I know he wants me to like her.

40

"Yeah, I mean it was a little embarrassing. Most of the people in the stands are media, coaches, football people."

"Don't forget the fan girls," I remind him, knowing that if they existed in high school, they certainly exist in college.

"Yeah." Jace shrugs. "And then my mom is there, smiling and waving at me." He doesn't have to tell me that any embarrassment he felt was washed away by the joy at having her there, for no other reason than to watch him. To show her support.

"So how was your night last night? You end up going out with your friends?" He switches the subject, unwilling to delve any farther into his relationship with Annie.

I shift in his lap, focusing on running my hands through his hair. I have to tell him about Wes and I don't want to.

"Parties are boring without you there." I'm stalling, letting my fingers graze down his back until they rest at his waistband.

Jace raises his lips in a smile, pleased I missed him, but wondering if I'll elaborate. If he should be worried for any reason. Always ready to worry about me.

"I talked to Wes last night," I finally say.

Jace sits up straighter, sensing that I have something important to tell him. "Yeah?"

"He's not going to Princeton. At least not this year," I amend when Jace's arms tighten around me. He worries about Wes too.

41

"What? Why?"

I tell him as best I can about Wes's rant last night, and I can feel Jace growing restless. He stands up, placing me on his desk, and paces around his tiny dorm room. His hands go to his hair and he pulls at it, the ultimate sign that my news is stressing him out. Majorly. I don't know what I expected. Maybe surprise, confusion, and then happiness that Wes would still be around instead of on the other side of the country. But there's a lot more going on here. Jace is wired, and I'm not sure why he's reacting so dramatically. He's usually all action, but I can tell he doesn't know what to do right now. His emotions are overwhelming him.

There's a bang at the door.

"Yo! Wilder!" Frankie's voice booms from the other side.

Jace opens the door and though his back is to me, based on Frankie's reaction, I imagine Jace looks fairly worked up.

"Uh, hi Pepper," Frankie waves, his voice as big and booming as his huge frame. I don't know if I'll ever get used to the enormity of this guy. "We gotta grab dinner before our individual meetings with coaches. You're up first so..."

Jace sighs and rubs his hands over his head again. He's got two or three workouts a day plus all kinds of various meetings. It's not going to be easy spending time together. Once classes start, it will only get worse.

"But that means you'll be done first, too," Frankie points out with a grin and a wink in my direction.

"Thanks, man, now give me a fucking minute, will you?" he says good-naturedly, letting Frankie know the tension in the room is not directed at him. He pushes Frankie, who has eased his way in the room, back out into the common area and shuts the door. We can hear Frankie's booming laughter from the other side.

"I want you to stay here and wait for me, but that'd be shitty of me to ask." Jace sits on the edge of the bed, looking at me intently. I'm not sure why he can't ask me that.

He must read the question in my expression because he says, "I'd feel like an asshole having you sit in this lame room for two hours bored out of your mind until I come back. I'll drive you home."

I'm disappointed. I thought Frankie just said he'd be done early.

"I should see Wes after my meeting," Jace explains as he leans over to grab his keys from his dresser. It's like he can read my mind. "We need to talk. Can I come over to your place after?"

"Sure," I say without hesitation. It will be late by then, but I'm unwilling to miss out on seeing him again.

My body is aching for rest, and after a quick shower and dinner of chicken noodle casserole with Gran, I crash hard. I only slept a couple of hours last night and my body greedily soaks up the shut-eye opportunity. Gran tells me in the morning that Jace stopped by around ten but they didn't want to wake me.

"The boy took off with our noodle casserole leftovers," Gran pretend-complains. I have little doubt she shoved it in his arms, worried that the college cafeteria food isn't up to her home-cooked standards, which I'm sure it isn't.

My quads are sore from lifting yesterday, not to mention my abs, back, arms... well, my whole body is sore. But I lace up anyway, confident that a run with Dave will get the blood flowing and loosen me up. Jace told me I'd eventually stop being sore after every weight lifting session, once I got stronger. But I keep ramping up the weights. What's the point in lifting if it doesn't push you past your limits?

After a good night's sleep, I feel a huge sense of relief settle in me as Dave and I hit the familiar dirt trail winding along the creek and into the woods. Jace was practically desperate to see me yesterday. I don't know what I was expecting. It's not like I really thought he'd suddenly lose interest in me after one day of college. But if I'm really honest with myself, that was a fear. That college life would consume him so thoroughly there simply wouldn't be room for me anymore.

When I get back from my morning run, I find the dining room table has been pushed against the wall, Gran is on all fours splayed out across a Twister mat, Zoe is leaning forward in an awkward split beneath her, and Kayla Chambers has the spinner in her hand calling out, "Left hand, yellow."

"Sugar boogers!" Gran huffs out as she twists onto her back in an effort to reach for the yellow circle.

"Oh, hey Pep!" Zoe calls out from underneath Gran's armpit.

"Ummm ..." I study them. "Hi?"

Kayla grins, clearly enjoying her role as the spinner. When she calls out, "Right foot blue," Gran and Zoe end up in a tangled heap, giggling like five year olds.

"This is my life," I tell Kayla, my hands up in resignation.

Kayla smiles and puts down the spinner. "I never knew Twister could be so entertaining. I may have to propose a Twister party to the Theta Kapp girls." She puckers her lips thoughtfully and I wonder if she's serious.

"Theta Kapp?" Zoe asks, rising from the ground and giving Gran a hand to help her up.

"Yeah, Theta Kappa Zeta is the sorority I'm pledging with. We just moved into the dorms two days ago. Same day as the athletes for preseason. But Heather, you know, my sister?" Zoe and I nod, but Kayla already knows we know Heather Chambers. Like Kayla, she was the most popular girl in her grade at Brockton Public. She's a junior at UC now. "She told me everything to expect and unless I do something totally wacky, I'll be a Theta Kapp sister in a few months."

UC has a pretty major Greek system, but I'm essentially clueless when it comes to that stuff. As far as I know, the women's cross team isn't part of a sorority, so it's really not on my radar.

Gran stretches her back and walks by me toward the front door, patting my cheek as she passes. "I'm off to Silver Sneakers with Lulu, ladies," she tells us, lacing up her purple Nikes, which match her purple velour sweat suit. Lulu is Gran's BFF and I'm thankful they have each other to look out for one another. "Nice to meet you, Kayla," Gran calls with a wave, already out the door on the way to the local recreation center for her fitness class.

"She's a busy woman," I comment with a shake of my head. I turn to Kayla, wondering when she'll explain her reason for being at my apartment. I didn't even know she knew where I lived. Well, I guess she knows I live on Jace's street, but still.

"How's Jace doing?" she asks instead. "I haven't really seen anyone on the football team yet because they're always practicing."

She sounds genuine, but I study her for an ulterior motive. It's unlikely she came all the way over here to check up on Jace.

"He's good, and yeah, they've pretty much had nonstop workouts and meetings since he got there." I open the fridge and pull out a jug of iced tea, raising it in question to Zoe and Kayla, who shake their heads.

"Well then, where have you been?" Zoe asks. "You never called me back yesterday."

Oops. Totally forgot about all those voicemails. And Kayla called yesterday too. My heart rate starts to pick up as it dawns on me that there might be something super important people have been trying to tell me. I need more than a couple hours of sleep if I'm supposed to have the energy to keep up with the world.

"Sorry, I had a lunch shift at the Tavern and then I stopped by to see Jace and then I fell asleep at, like, seven o'clock," I explain. "Give a girl a break, will you?" I taunt Zoe, who can be fairly dramatic when she's in the mood but never takes things too seriously.

"Yeah, I figured," she says with a shrug before stealing my glass and taking a swig.

"Hey! Get your own!"

I can feel Kayla watching us, and I wonder if she recognizes that she's out of place here in her hot pink shorts, white sleeveless button-down, and French manicured nails. I'm a sweaty mess and Zoe looks like she just rolled out of bed.

"How'd you get here, anyway?" I ask Zoe. "I didn't see the Burton mobile outside." Zoe usually gets around in the family minivan.

"I got a bike!" she tells me excitedly. "I went running with Jenny yesterday afternoon, since *you* never called me back," she feigns hurt, "and her parents were having a garage sale and just, like, gave me this old road bike for free. It's sweet. Lots of character."

Zoe and I banter back and forth for a few more minutes before I sense Kayla growing restless, waiting her turn to jump in.

"So what's up, Kayla?" I finally ask.

She smiles brightly. "Well, I wanted to invite you, both of you, to Theta Kapp's first party of the year," she announces with formality.

I stare at her blankly, and I imagine Zoe shares my confusion. When we don't react, she must realize we need further explanation.

"It's actually a pretty big deal," she informs us, leaning her hip against the counter. "Every August, Theta Kapp and Sig Beta – you know, the hottest frat at UC," she adds like it's an uncontroversial fact, which it might be, "throw the first major event of the school year. The only people on campus are the sororities, fraternities, and athletes for preseason. And sometimes some randoms but they don't usually get an invite," she adds dismissively. "The main point is to get goodwill going between the houses and the athletes."

This all makes sense, except it doesn't explain why Zoe and I should be there.

"Right, well, that's cool of you to think of us but we're not UC students, Kayla, so…" I let her reach her own conclusion. I'm not going to be someone who shows up where she doesn't belong. I'll be in college next year, and I can go to the party then.

But Kayla has zeroed in on Zoe, whose eyes are alight with excitement. "Are you kidding? This sounds awesome! Pepper, we are so going."

"We have the annual cross barbeque at Coach's place, remember?" I point out.

"Yeah, but that's over early enough. When do people show up for the party?" she asks Kayla.

"Most people start getting there around eight or nine. Earlier than a lot of parties because the athletes are worn out. But they'll rally. Most of the teams have hardcore practices the first few days and then the coaches give them the morning off after the party. It's tradition."

One thing I do know is that sororities and fraternities are all about tradition. I'm sure Jace will be there, but I'm not so sure he'd want me along. I don't want to invade his space.

Not to mention… "Our first day of school is the next day." Yeah, there's no way Zoe's getting away with going to that party, and even Gran won't be down with it.

Zoe doesn't look fazed. "I've already got a sneak-out plan ready to implement," she says proudly. "I figure I can only lie about so many sleepovers with you before my parents get suspicious." It doesn't surprise me that Zoe is planning on going to a lot of parties this year. But I don't have much interest in joining her.

Zoe and Kayla chat on about the party but I zone them out. It's dawning on me that senior year without Jace might be lonely for entirely different reasons than I originally feared. If I want to be the national cross champion again, I'm not going to be spending as much time with Zoe, who seems to have a completely different agenda than mine. She's not even sure if she'll run competitively in college.

Kayla became our friend over the past year, but I don't entirely believe she's invited us to this important semi-exclusive college thing simply because we hang out occasionally. My presence must give her, or her sorority, some sort of power, and I'm sure it has to do with Jace. Who knows the inner workings of college Greek life and how a girl like me might matter in their games? Does Zoe realize we're just pawns to them?

Kayla seems somewhat surprised that I'm not more flattered by her invitation. Her reaction just shows that she really doesn't know me that well. I finally realize the girls won't give up on convincing me to go until I at least give them something more than a flat-out no way. Eventually a vague, "We'll see," gets them out the door.

I only did a five-mile loop this morning but my legs are trashed. I suppose it wouldn't hurt to take some Ryan Harding medicine and rest tomorrow, but I'm reluctant to give up my 84-day streak of not taking a day off from running. Besides, we usually do our first semi-long run as a team before the season kick-off barbeque tomorrow. And I'm not planning on sitting it out.

I'm rummaging through the freezer looking for something to ice my aches and pains with when the front door – still partially open from the girls leaving a moment earlier – swings wide open. "Pepper!" Wes calls before seeing me only a few feet away, a bag of frozen peas in my hand.

"Oh, hi you." He leans in for a hug, despite my state of post-run stink.

"What hurts?" he asks when we break away, eyeing my bag of peas. Only athletes are familiar with the real purpose behind frozen peas.

"Everything," I answer.

"You should take an ice bath," he suggests.

"That sounds like a form of medieval torture." I grimace just thinking about a bath full of ice. Only if I'm in so much pain I couldn't walk would I put myself through that.

"Or we could go to the creek for a swim. It's pretty fucking cold." Wes is grinning, and I can't help but grin back, happy he's emerged from the emotional turmoil I witnessed the other night.

Perhaps it's because I know it's just beneath his fun-loving exterior, all the anxiety and hurt he suppresses, that I say, "Sure, why not?" I almost never hang out with Wes without Jace, but we used to a long time ago, and it's not so hard to remember that easy friendship that wasn't complicated by me and Jace being, well, the so-much-more than friends that we are today.

It feels even weirder when Wes stops by Jace's house to borrow a pair of swim trunks. This isn't going to become, like, a thing, is it? Me and Wes hanging out without Jace. Why do things keep changing in ways I don't expect?

Chapter 6

For some reason, on the way to the creek, I'm under the false impression that no one else will be at the swimming hole. It's still early in the day, and when Jace is off immersed in football I sometimes feel like the rest of world is momentarily on hold too. But that's definitely just my imagination because there are at least a dozen other cars at what I always thought was a fairly secretive spot.

A part of me is relieved. Though we aren't doing anything wrong, it just feels disloyal to hang in my bathing suit with another guy. Even if it *is* with Wes, who's like family. I never asked him why he showed up at my apartment in the first place. We haven't been on stopping-by-unannounced-terms since middle school. I guess he's stopped by without plans before when he's with Jace, but that's different. Or is it? Maybe I'm overanalyzing everything, but I just get a feeling Jace wouldn't like it.

Wes stops us at the top of the trail leading down to the creek. We look over the ledge and take in the series of swimming holes. The water is clear and enticing.

"It's all guys down there," I point out as I take in the absence of bikinis and ponytails.

Judging by the size of the bodies below, I'm assuming it's UC students. I'm glad it's no one I know, I'm not really in the mood to be social. I'm too exhausted and all I want is the cold water to ease my achy legs and then I was hoping for a snooze by the creek with the warm sun heating the rocks and my skin. At the sight of a keg and the loud laughter coming from below, my napping plans go out the window.

"It's just Sig Beta guys," Wes says, his tense shoulders relaxing. I wonder if he still worries about running into Wolfe or Rex, ghosts from his drug-dealing past.

"Sig Beta?"

"Yeah, they're hosting that party with Kayla's sorority tomorrow night."

"How do you know about that?"

"I ran into Kayla and Zoe outside your place," he admits. "I'm supposed to convince you to show up." Wes chuckles and throws his arm around me. I love that he won't try to make me do something he knows I don't want to. "You don't have to go but I'm totally hitting that up. Theta Kapp girls are smoking."

I roll my eyes and take in the tan muscled bodies as we reach the creek. That's right. Sig Beta are the hottest guys on campus, according to Kayla, who probably meant to imply that her sorority has the hottest girls.

"Well, you should take Zoe then. That way maybe she won't give me a hard time for staying home."

"Yeah, no problem," Wes agrees before swiping my towel and pushing me in the deepest swimming hole with one fluid movement. *How did I not see earlier that Jace and Wes are brothers?* I think, as the icy cold water hits me. Both are freakishly smooth and athletic in their movements. Sneaky, as well. I rise to the surface sputtering.

"You little shit!" I say between gasps. The cold water has taken my breath away. But I don't get out of the water.

53

Wes and I realize at the same moment that about twenty heads have turned our way and they all seem to be staring at me. There's no way I'm getting out in my polka-dotted string bikini, shivering, I might add.

My heart is already racing from the sneak attack and freezing water, but it picks up another notch when my eyes skate over Clayton Dennison. I pretend not to notice that I've spotted him as I tread water and return my focus to Wes. Clayton's eyes are shaded by a baseball cap and I can't tell if he was looking my way.

Baseball doesn't have preseason because their main competitive season is in the spring. So I guess he's just hanging out with his fraternity friends. But really, it's a huge school, how is it possible to run into him twice in as many days?

A guy is making his way over to Wes, who's hanging our towels over a branch.

"Jamison, what's up, man?" a voice I recognize but can't place greets him.

"Gage, hey," Wes sounds significantly less pleased to see him. Gage Fitzgerald. The annoying fraternity president who helped, or tried to help, Jace move in to his dorm.

I dive under the water, irritated that I can't escape this college world, a world which was so distant to me only a few days ago. As I make my way to the bottom of the creek, grabbing a stone and pushing back up to the surface, I wonder why I'm irritated. Isn't it a good thing to be part of Jace's new life? Maybe, but if it means hanging out with the Gage Fitzgeralds of the world, I'm not exactly thrilled. I slowly break the surface again, hoping everyone will forget I'm here so I can find a discreet rock to sunbathe on.

But I'm not so lucky.

Clayton has appeared beside Gage, says something I can't hear, and all three pairs of eyes turn to look at me. Wes's mood is rapidly declining. An internal warning light flashes.

Instead of rescuing him from two guys he clearly doesn't want to talk to – if his body language is any indication – I wait as long as I can in the creek, swimming over to a ledge where I can sort of sit while keeping most of my body under water. I try to ignore the fraternity guys glancing in our direction, but it's hard when I'm also trying to ignore the freezing cold water. Eventually I start to go numb, and that helps. After all, it's good for my achy legs. A group of guys farther down the creek are talking and gesturing toward Wes, Gage, and Clayton. I wonder if they know Wes, and if so, why.

Clayton's from Brockton and even though Wes went to the private school – Lincoln Academy – instead of Brockton Public, their acquaintance isn't surprising. They are both athletes and their paths were bound to cross. And Gage... he seems to be the kind of guy who tries to know everyone who might matter, and I guess even in high school Wesley Jamison had important status. After all, he was the Jace Wilder of Lincoln Academy: the leader of the social scene, the best athlete, hottest guy, yada yada.

Eventually the three seem engrossed in conversation enough for me to risk grabbing my towel without attracting attention. Remembering a spot farther up the trail that Jace took me to a few weeks ago, I slip on my flip-flops and snag my towel from the branch before heading that way. But the conversation stops when they see me, and in an effort not to be super rude, I turn and wave before bee-lining back to the trail.

I'm lying on my back on the warm rocks when Wes joins me a few minutes later.

"You didn't tell me you met Gage Fitzgerald." He sounds angry, and I'm on the defensive.

"Uh, yeah, he had some pledges try to help move Jace in the other day. What's the problem?"

"He's a prick." Wes's voice is contemptuous.

"Yeah, that's obvious. Do you guys have a history or something?" Wes hangs out with social-climbers like Gage all the time and they usually don't bother him, so there must be more to it.

"I used to sell him drugs," Wes explains matter-of-factly. "He doesn't like his new dealer and wants me back in the business. And he likes that my dad has connections. So he wants to be my buddy, you know how that goes."

"He does drugs?" I ask, wide-eyed. I mean, I'm not totally naïve about these things. I know a lot of people do drugs, but Gage comes across as a pretty clean-cut dude.

"I guess. I think he bought a lot for his fraternity brothers. He was like a sub-dealer, I guess you'd call him. Sold at parties and shit. Probably didn't do a lot himself. Or maybe he did. I don't really give a shit."

That makes more sense. I don't see him as a regular user. He has his shit together too much for that. Some people deal for money, others for power and control, or both. Not that I've known a ton of drug dealers, but it doesn't take a genius to figure out their motives. Gage probably falls into the latter category.

"And Clayton Dennison? Is he in Sig Beta?"

Wes's head swings from looking toward the creek back to me. "He's a prick too, Pepper. You know that, right?"

"I don't really know him," I respond honestly with a shrug. He's never come off as an arrogant asshole like Gage Fitzgerald did on first impression, but I'm suspicious of Clayton given his history with Jace.

"He's not a Sig Beta brother," Wes gets back to my question. "But Sig Beta is kind of like the frat for UC athletes to hang with. Only athletes on the major sports, no offense to cross, Pep."

I laugh. I can't help it. It's a relief cross country is not as popular as football or baseball. And it's not news to me.

Wes smiles too, and I hope his mood turns back to happy. I'm not used to him being moody like this.

"Sports teams don't have time to be in their own frat or sorority, so they just mooch?" I ask.

"Pretty much," Wes says. "It's what we call a symbiotic relationship," he tells me with a grin. "The athletes get the benefits of the parties and social stuff but don't have to do any of the work, and the frats get the benefit of having all the hot athletes at their events, making them more popular."

"Makes sense." But I don't like it. If it means Jace will be hanging with the Sig Beta guys, I have a bad feeling.

The guys don't bother us anymore, and after a couple hours napping in the sun, Wes drops me off at home. He offers to come in and wait while I change for my shift at the Tavern, but Gran's already planning on giving me a ride. I've got my license, but no car.

It's my last shift at the Tavern until next summer. It's a decent place to work, and I got promoted from bus girl to hostess this summer. Another plus is that my teammate Jenny Mendoza started working here this year. She'll only be a sophomore and stands at 4'10" but she's got enough spunk to make up for her littleness.

The restaurant's busy, as usual, which makes the night fly by. Just when things are starting to slow down, a group of guys and girls walk in. They look college-aged, and I'm a little surprised they've chosen the Tavern as a place to hang out at ten at night. It's a nice restaurant, and we don't usually see a lot of college kids, unless they're on a date or with family.

When an especially tall guy maneuvers to the front of the group, I realize there might be another reason for their presence.

Clayton's cleaned up from the creek earlier, and it looks like he's ditched the fraternity guys in favor of fellow athletes. When he feigns surprise at seeing me and then attempts a hug, I can't help but scowl at him.

He pretends not to notice. "Man, I've run into you a lot over the last couple of days, Pepper. I'm a lucky guy."

"You guys headed to the bar or do you want a table?" I ask, ignoring his comment.

"We'll take a table." He circles his hand around his friends. "For eight."

The restaurant is emptying, and a large circular booth is available. I lead them to it, and pull up two chairs on the end so the whole party can fit. I can feel Clayton's gaze burning into the back of my head. Though it could just be a coincidence that he's here, I doubt it. It's not a stretch that he knows I work here, since I've been working at the Tavern every summer in high school.

Before I can escape, Clayton begins introducing me to all of his friends, acting as though the two of us are old buddies from high school. I try to step away from the hand he places on the small of my back, a gesture he's surely aware demonstrates a familiarity we do not possess.

Two of the girls are on the soccer team and the other two play softball. The three other guys are baseball players. Each of them is attractive, and I have no doubt they hold some social clout at UC. That's why he brought them and why he's putting on this show. He wants people who matter talking about me with him. He wants to get underneath Jace Wilder's skin.

He's sneaky but not subtle enough for me. I discovered what he was up to years ago at Brockton Public, and apparently he's still at it.

When I return to the hostess table, Jenny's reaction tells me that his plan is so-far successful. Now doing my old job, she passes me with a bucket of dishes. I'm not on her route to the kitchen, and I know what she's there for when she pauses, balancing the bucket on her hip.

"Pepper! Do you know who that is?" she asks with hero-worship written all over her face. "My brothers and dad have been making me watch Clayton Dennison's baseball games forever! I can't believe you know him. And it seems like you guys are pretty close. Can you introduce me?"

59

Sighing, I take the bucket from Jenny and carry it into the kitchen. "We're not friends. I hardly know the guy."

"Well, he wants to be your friend. He was totally checking out your ass when you were taking them to the table, and he put his arm on you that way guys do when they're telling other guys you're taken."

"How do you even know that kind of thing, Jenny? You're fifteen and never had a boyfriend." I'm not trying to be insulting, but sometimes Jenny seems more knowledgeable about the ways of the world than I am, and I've got two years on her. I'm genuinely curious about how she knows these things.

She shrugs. "Older siblings, I guess."

A waiter is taking their orders when Jenny and I come back from the kitchen, but I can still feel Clayton watching us.

"God, Pepper. You must cast some sort of spell over hot guys. You've already got Jace Wilder and now Clayton Dennison is looking at you like he wants to eat you up."

I can't help the laughter that bursts out upon hearing my eighty-pound friend say the words "eat you up" in a sexual context.

"Would you stop?" I try to sound serious through my laughter. I'm not going to go into the whole reason behind Clayton's presence here, and his pretend interest in me. "Seriously, Jenny, it's nothing."

I'm hoping if I just ignore the guy he'll realize he can't get to Jace through me. As the hostess, I'm able to hang out away from his table, especially now that the crowds have slowed down. But then Jenny goes to clear the dishes from Clayton's table, and she remains there for nearly ten minutes. It takes some willpower not to intervene. Based on the giggling coming from Jenny, there's no doubt Clayton is charming her.

When she finally heads into the kitchen with their dishes, I corner her. She's grinning widely. "They invited me to hang out with them afterward!" she announces.

My mouth goes dry. "You aren't actually thinking of going, are you?"

"What? Of course I'm going to go! I'll probably be grounded for a month, but it's worth it. This is *Clayton Dennison*. They invited you too. You'll come, right?"

Do I tell her he only invited her to make me come too? Because there's no way I'm letting Jenny go hang out late at night with a bunch of college students by herself. I don't know these people and they could be total creeps.

"I'm not going, Jenny, and you aren't either," I say in my most authoritative voice.

"Oh, come on, Pepper, don't be a party pooper."

"This isn't worth getting grounded for a month over, Jenny," I try to convince her.

"It is to me. And honestly, if my dad finds out it's Clayton Dennison I was with, he probably won't give me a very hard time."

Sighing, I decide I'll have to let her know there's more to this invitation. "Look, Clayton's trying to undermine Jace by hanging out with me. He probably invited you because he saw us talking, figured we were friends, and thought I'd go if you did."

"Really?" Jenny gives me a sidelong glance. I'm not one to make up stories like this, and she knows it. "Why's he want to undermine Jace?"

"That's more complicated. But just trust me on this."

She studies me. "I believe you. I mean, it makes more sense than him actually wanting to hang out with me." She doesn't sound disappointed, just thoughtful.

"So, you won't go?"

"Well, I'm not going without you, and if what you say is true, you shouldn't go." And then she gets a smug look. "It'll feel pretty good turning down Clayton Dennison." She rolls back her shoulders before heading back onto the floor.

That's my girl.

Chapter 7

The first day of school is weird. I think my best girlfriend has been elevated to the most popular girl in school, or at least a contender for that position. Wes took Zoe to the party that Kayla invited us to. Wes is a pretty big deal, and going to a college party, especially an invite-only one that's fairly exclusive, is a really big deal. So, now Zoe Burton is a big deal.

Zoe and I have been friends since freshman year, and I know she didn't seek out this social status. She probably didn't even see it coming. But the girl likes to have fun. And I have to say, she's easing into the role of popular girl pretty well.

We sit at the senior popular table at lunch. It's not my first time at this table, I've been here with Jace and his friends before. But now it's with Zoe, Omar, Rollie, and yeah, some others I'm not really friends with, but for the most part, it's *my* group at the popular table. I don't like it.

Zoe and I sit by the window, and she turns to face me, blocking everyone else out. "Pep, I have seriously been trying to talk to you, alone, for like, three days," she says in a low voice.

"Shit, sorry." I've been cursing a lot since spending more time with Jace and Wes. Well, not a lot, but more than usual.

"You are gossip-clueless so I need to fill you in because it's almost old news and everyone's gonna assume you know," she says without a breathing-break. "Ryan broke up with Lisa."

"Oh?" I make the mistake of glancing over Zoe's shoulder and find Dana and Tina watching us. They're at the other end of the table though, so I don't think they can hear us.

"Yeah, I found out at Dana's party the other night. It happened right after you left. I had no idea news can spread that fast. Everyone at the party was talking about it and I wanted to talk to you because... your name came up a few times."

That gets my attention. "What? Why?"

Ryan and I dated for a few months last fall. We were good together but, well, I was in love with Jace. Still. Always. But Lisa had a thing for Ryan ever since he moved here for his senior year, and they got together almost as quickly as Jace and I did after we broke up. So no hard feelings... not really.

"Lisa thinks he's still into you," Zoe whispers. She's not always so discreet, so I appreciate her effort. "He said it was because they were starting college, which is lame, because they're both at UC. That he would be busy with running, didn't think they should try to stay together when they'd both have a lot going on... Total bullshit really."

"I'm glad you said that," I tell her with a nod. Because those reasons apply to me and Jace and *we* aren't breaking up.

"Anyway, people are talking, you know? It'll blow over. But, aside from you and Jace, they were the hottest couple here and going to UC together and everything? People like to turn it into drama. Just don't let it get to you." She pats me on the shoulder and steals a grape from my Tupperware. Gran still packs me lunch.

This is why I love Zoe. She listens to gossip, and might even perpetuate it at times, but she doesn't take it seriously. She sees it for what it is.

Gazing out the window, I recall Ryan's dejected look when I saw him on his way to the gym. That was the morning after he broke up with Lisa. So he was definitely sad, right? Shaking my head, I bite into my peanut butter and banana sandwich. It doesn't matter. It *can't* matter. This is just gossip. After nearly a year, and most of that with both of us in relationships, Ryan Harding cannot still have feelings for me.

But I remember that he left me a voicemail later that day. I never called him back. The message said I didn't need to. But it was the kind of message that made me feel like there was something he wanted to talk to me about, but knew maybe he shouldn't and was sort of glad I hadn't answered the phone. And that's why I never called him back. After hearing this news, I have the feeling I made the right decision on that one.

***

When I toe the line for the first cross meet of the season, I'm amazed how quickly it's arrived. The first few weeks of my senior year have been a whirlwind. I've managed to get in three weight lifting sessions before school each week, but that means I have to go to bed pretty early. So after school it's practice, rush home to eat dinner and maybe do like five minutes of homework, and then rush to UC to spend some time with Jace, if I can.

Between my homework and Jace's football commitments, we don't see each other every night, which sucks, but I'm grateful he's still making an effort to fit me in. Fortunately, my classes this semester aren't very tough, and Jace is taking the classes recommended by his coaches, which pretty much means he has no homework. But he tries to see his mom with some of his free time, and he's already been out of town for two games in the past month.

Things have been crazy busy but good between Jace and me. Some of my fears have completely disappeared. Both of us are so focused on training that we don't want to party. Jace doesn't talk about it, but I can tell from his roommates' comments that his teammates give him a hard time for bailing on parties. It's not very heartfelt though. I think his teammates respect that he takes training so seriously, and they know him being in good form is key to the team's success. Ironically, Jace hasn't played in a game yet. The coaches didn't think he was ready and didn't want to risk injury for the first couple of pre-season games. He's playing for the first time tonight, a home game. He got box tickets for me, Gran, Jim, Jim's girlfriend Sheila, and his mom, Annie.

But here I am, at my first meet, and Jace is watching with Gran. I don't feel much anxiety at all. This is the third time I've run this course, and I know I'm in amazing shape. I've been smashing the workouts. The boys can't even keep up with me. All I really feel is confidence.

I didn't race this meet last year. Coach thought I needed to hold back since the championship meets go so late in the season, and I'd be too tired if I started racing in September. But I'm a more mature runner now, and after chatting with Coach Tom, I convinced him that racing at all the meets was wise. I love racing. And I'll get bored and antsy if I don't race.

But now I'm one mile in, running alone, and I'm actually slightly bored. I knew beforehand this wasn't a very competitive race. But I don't even feel like I'm racing. I can't hear anyone behind me. I've been running to the point of pain and exhaustion so regularly these days that one more run like that doesn't faze me. Yeah, my legs are tired. Yeah, I feel the burn. But that's nothing new.

The boys' team pauses in their warm up as I run by – they race after us – and their cheering encourages me to keep pushing harder. This *is* a race, after all.

"Dude, she's like half a mile ahead of the next girl," I hear one of the guys say.

When I emerge from the woods and hit the final stretch across a soccer field, Gran is jumping up and down like I'm in a shoulder-to-shoulder finish in a major race. For her, I kick it up a notch and push harder. Her enthusiasm is contagious. Jace is there too, calling my name and making me want to dig deep.

When I cross the finish line and see my time flash in front of me, my heart practically stops. 16:36. *No way.*

That's the fastest time I've ever run a 5K. I wrack my brain, trying to remember if this course has a reputation for being fast, or if it is actually a shorter distance than the typical course. But no, I don't recall any of that. My time is faster than I've run at any championship meet, and I didn't even need to push hard to win. Glancing behind me, no one else has even emerged from the woods yet.

But as Gran and Jace rush toward me, the boys' team not far behind, I don't feel like celebrating. That was too fast. Too soon. Nationals isn't for three more months and judging by the quiver in my legs... not to mention the pain in my shins I've been ignoring for weeks, I'm not sure I can maintain this level of fitness for much longer. When I glance up and see Coach Tom, who is smiling at me, but looks worried, I know I'm right. Shit.

***

"To breaking records!" Gran exclaims, raising her shot glass to clink with mine.

The whiskey burns my throat as it slides down and I can feel it spread heat throughout my chest and belly. Gran squeals with glee at my disgusted expression before pouring herself another. She knows better than to pour a second for me.

Gran can't understand why I'm not super-happy about my race this morning. My mood on race days is usually directly correlated with my performance. And today's performance will go down in history. Hell, I've never run that fast in my life. The reason I'm acting like a "sullen teenager" (Gran's words) is because I'm afraid I'll never run that fast again. At least not this season. I don't know what to do now. Do I push through it? Train even harder than before? Or do I back off now and pick it up again closer to championship season? I know I should talk to Coach Tom, who must suspect I've been doing extra workouts, but I don't want to see the disappointment on his face.

With the whiskey that Gran convinced me to drink making me feel warm and fuzzy, I start to feel like maybe it will all be okay. Maybe I will just keep breaking course records every meet. Maybe I'll be on fire straight through until Nationals.

Jim and Sheila drive us to Jace's football game and the four of us meet Annie in our boxed seats. Annie and Jim were so young when they had Jace, and Annie's drug addiction was such a clear-cut reason for their breakup, that the two of them have this amicable, non-awkward relationship. Sheila doesn't seem to mind Annie on the few occasions we've all been together, and I imagine enough time has passed that Annie's no longer a threat to Sheila and Jim's relationship.

Jace's jersey isn't available for fans to purchase yet, so I've got on his old Brockton Public jersey with a UC baseball cap to show my acknowledgement that, yes, I know he's not still in high school.

The "Wilder" on the back of the jersey attracts some attention, but I wear it with confidence, because Jace and I have held it together for over a month since he started college. And we haven't even been rattled – not much, at least.

Gran is in rare form tonight after two shots of whiskey. Always an enthusiastic fan, she's hoarse by half time. It's the most fun I've had in a while. I love watching Jace play football, but I've never watched a game as his girlfriend. We started dating right after his last high school season ended. In the past, I've been surrounded by other girls vying for him and I thought I couldn't have him beyond our friendship. But now I'm secluded from other girls with family, and he belongs to all of us. The pride we share as he throws another awesome pass vibrates amongst us.

By the time the game ends, I'm not only beaming with pride but I'm also feeling slightly hot and bothered – definitely not a good thing when I'm with Jace's parents and my Gran. Fortunately, they head out and leave me to meet up with Jace alone.

I'm not surprised to see the players' families and friends waiting outside the locker room, but the press with cameras and microphones at the ready remind me that UC just won their first home game – by twenty-four points – to a team they haven't beaten in years. My heart sinks, realizing it might be awhile before I get Jace alone.

He finally comes outside with a large group of players, looking both adorable and tough with damp hair from a shower and wearing jeans and a tee shirt. His eyes search the crowd and when they land on me, he flashes a smile that quite literally has my knees buckling. I grab the fence next to me, prepared to wait as the reporters approach him. But he tells them he won't be doing any interviews and walks straight through them to me.

He doesn't kiss me, just takes my hand. "Hi," he says quietly. "Wanna get out of here?"

Do I ever.

Chapter 8

An hour later and full of pizza we had delivered, we're snuggling on Jace's bed, contemplating returning to a puzzle we started a few days ago or watching a movie, when we hear the door to the main entry swing open and loud male voices enter the common area. Jace's door is closed but a moment later there's loud banging.

"Are you decent in there, Wilder?" the voice roars. It's not one I recognize.

"He's with Pepper, give them a minute," Frankie says.

Jace rolls his eyes to the ceiling. "I had a feeling this might happen."

"Who is it?"

"Turner," Jace tells me as he swings his legs off the bed, resigned. There's more banging. Chandler Turner is one of the UC football team captains.

Jace opens the door to three huge guys as I quickly sit up on the bed. They all look at me and I wave sheepishly.

"What?" Jace asks. Although I suspect he already knows. And I have a feeling I know too. Jace has managed to avoid going out to any parties so far. He's either hanging out with me or the team is out of town for an away game.

"Dude, I get you want to hang with your girl, but you gotta celebrate with the team." Turner's arms are crossed and he's nearly as large as Frankie, who is standing behind him, looking a little guilty. Frankie must have let them in, but judging by the determined look on the upperclassmen football players' faces, I don't blame him.

"You can bring her," a junior who I recognize as Dimitri Johnson, says, nodding in my direction. "Hi Pepper, we've never met because your boyfriend keeps you to himself, but I'm Dimitri."

"And I'm Chandler," Turner adds. "You need to get your boy to come out after such a big win."

"Everyone's asking for you, man. Your absence is bringing down morale," Dimitri says, laying it on thick. Frankie just shrugs silently behind them, helpless.

"Bringing down morale?" Jace scoffs. But he knows what they mean. He's become the face of the team, and he needs to represent. Jace is a natural leader, even as a freshman, and hiding away in his dorm room with me is simply unacceptable. He might not need to party as hard as he did in high school, but he's got to make a showing.

Jace has already slipped on his shoes and he hands me my cowboy boots. I raise my eyebrows. "I've been up since 5:30 this morning, Jace." It's a weak protest, and I actually want to go with, just so I know what's going on. But I also don't want to intrude on team stuff if Jace doesn't want me tagging along, so I leave the decision to him, not wanting him to feel obligated to bring me.

"I thought you took a nap after the race?" he asks. And that's enough of a green light. He wants me by his side.

"Yeah, yeah," I concede, pulling on my boots. I slept for three hours in the middle of the day. With the hulks watching us from the doorway, I relent and let Jace take my hand and pull me off the bed.

"Let's go," he says.

We pile into Chandler Turner's car and he drives us a few minutes across campus. I'm squeezed in between Frankie and Jace in the back seat and for some reason, being crammed in a car with four large dudes helps diminish my anxiety about the party.

I'm pretty sure I know why Jace has been putting it off. One time Frankie was giving him a hard time about it, and teased him that he'd protect him from the hordes of girls. I thought he'd been partially joking, or at least exaggerating. But as we emerge from the car and make our way toward the crowds of people outside on a lawn, the number of eyes turning our way, mostly female, is alarming. It must be because we're with the captain of the football team. Surely, once we've separated from Chandler and Dimitri, the girls I can feel following behind us (it takes all my effort not to look) will disappear.

Jace slides his arm around my waist. "I'm glad you're still wearing my jersey," he leans in to tell me.

"You're telling me," I reply dryly.

We follow Turner and Dimitri to a fire pit. "You guys want a drink?" Frankie offers. We decline, but Frankie leaves us to find the keg.

When we settle amongst a group around the fire, I finally take in the scene around me. Stricken by the size of the guys at the party, I realize I've never actually been in one place with Jace's entire team before. "I'm surrounded by giants," I murmur.

Jace chuckles. "Basketball and baseball guys are here too. It's a lot of big guys."

"And girls," I murmur, noticing one in particular manning the keg who towers over some of the guys. She eyes me up and down as she pours a beer. "Who are all the girls?"

Jace shrugs, like he didn't even notice there were girls here. "Don't know."

My gaze lingers on the tall girl by the keg. She looks familiar, and when her eyes dart our way again between pours, I realize she was one of the girls with Clayton when he came to the Tavern the other night. That must explain why she won't stop staring at me. And Jace, it doesn't escape my notice. Though she's not the only girl doing this.

The number of people around the fire pit rapidly increases. Jace is eventually crowded by other guys – teammates or other athletes, most of them congratulating him on the game and offering him a drink. He introduces me to everyone, letting them know I'm his girlfriend, but I feel out of place. This is Jace's time to shine and I feel like a burden. Would he be having more fun without me? The girls won't stop ogling him, and their interest in me turns hostile as Jace continues to ignore them. But Jace keeps tugging me closer and offering brief kisses on my head, reassuring me that he prefers me at his side. Holding me to him like an anchor. And I sigh into that thought, trying to let go of the negative doubts that infiltrate whenever he's on display like this. Will I ever get used to it?

"Pepper!" Someone calls my name and I glance around before finding Kayla Chambers waving enthusiastically from the front porch of a house. "Hey! Hi guys!" she continues shouting as she makes her way toward us.

Heads swing in her direction and I get the feeling she's purposefully attracting attention.

When she leans in to give Jace a hug, I realize she's the only girl who's approached him all night, despite how many have lurked at our periphery. Interesting. Maybe I look more intimidating than I feel.

Kayla and Jace hung out on a regular basis throughout high school, and I know they've shared memories with mutual friends that I wasn't a part of. I'm okay with that. What bothers me is that Kayla also shares intimate memories with him. Jace was with a lot of girls before me, and I know none of them were serious. But still, the jealousy is there. And it's worse that she probably slept with him, and, well, we haven't done that together yet.

Kayla hugs me, too, but it doesn't escape my notice that she went straight for Jace. I don't suspect she's trying to pull a move on him or anything, she knows us well enough to know we're in a serious relationship, but I'm not stupid. Hugging Jace Wilder just elevated her social status to a whole new level. She's not just a hot freshman sorority girl anymore. Now she's one with power.

Before Jace and I got together, Kayla annoyed me like you might expect the most popular girl in her grade who's buddies with my crush would annoy me. But once I got to know her, she was cooler than I expected. And she had my back when Madeline Brescoll tried to get between me and Jace. Despite that, my guard is up right now. She's pledging with a sorority and as a freshman she's got something to prove. It's not like she's got her status established at the top of the food chain like she did at Brockton Public.

Warily, I hug her back, but I'm sure my face shows my suspicions because she looks away from me, back to Jace, smiling broadly. Jace isn't stupid either, and I feel his arm tighten around me.

"What's up, Kayla?" he asks in a tone that indicates his question is more than casual.

"You gu-uys!" she sing-songs. "You aren't having enough fun! So serious. Why don't you come on into the house and I can show you around?"

"We're good out here," Jace says. I glance at the house I hadn't paid attention to before, realizing this must be the home of Theta Kapp.

"You sure? We've got something that will ensure a *really* good night," she says, lowering her voice and wiggling her eyebrows knowingly.

She should know better. I glare at her. "Seriously, Kayla?"

I've never done drugs before and Jace hasn't in nearly a year. Not to get all self-righteous here, but Jace definitely can't afford *that* kind of partying with the spotlight on him. Not to mention all the other reasons.

Kayla straightens up, and I notice her pupils are dilated. "Chill, Pepper. We're discreet." Her voice is condescending, and I don't like it. "Besides, Jace wouldn't be the only one on his team letting loose after a great game."

"That's not very discreet, now, is it?" Jace's voice is low with suppressed anger.

"Jeez, Jace, you used to be so much fun," she huffs and then her eyes widen when she takes in our expressions. She's gone too far. And she knows it.

"What are you trying to say?" I'm not afraid to stand up for myself anymore. If she wants to hash this out, I'm game.

Her stuttering is interrupted by Gage Fitzgerald, who throws his arm around Kayla. "Kayla bear!" he greets her jovially. "Let's not forget we have an audience," he says quietly in her ear before looking pointedly at me and then Jace.

An audience doesn't bother me. We're not saying anything I'm uncomfortable with others overhearing. But Kayla blanches under Gage's arm.

Speaking loudly now, Gage says to Jace, "Hey man, ran into your pal Wes the other day."

I'm back on alert, not liking the way he said *pal*. That was weeks ago. Where is he going with this?

Jace remains silent, refusing to encourage Gage.

"He was at the creek with your girl, here." Gage nods at me. He's testing Jace for a reaction, and fortunately Jace doesn't give him one. He's better at reining it in than he used to be. Besides, I already told Jace about that excursion. He didn't seem thrilled, and I didn't feel right about it either, so I've tried to avoid one-on-one hanging out with Wes since.

"Are you trying to imply something?" Jace sounds threatening, and I'm happy he's forced Gage to get right to the point. He doesn't do well at pretending to be nice. Or oblivious for that matter. Gage wants something, and he might as well let us know what it is.

Frankie has joined us, and when I glance at him it registers that he's protective of me and Jace. Or maybe just Jace, and me by association. It's reassuring, and even though I don't know him very well, I trust him for some reason. He looks like a bodyguard standing there, legs wide, arms crossed, buzz cut and serious expression aimed at Gage.

I almost let out a giggle, but instead I just smile and nod at Frankie, who lets down his warrior attitude for a moment to wink at me.

Gage has backed off a little from his cocky tone. He raises his hands in a "take it easy" gesture. "I'm not implying anything, Wilder. If you're cool with Pepper here sunbathing in a string bikini with another guy, or a whole bunch of other guys as it turned out, then..."

He doesn't get to finish his sentence. Jace lets go of me so fast I almost lose my balance. But before he can throw a punch, Frankie is there, holding him back and telling him to think about what he's doing.

"You heard what the fucker said," Jace says through clenched teeth.

"Yeah, and it'll be all over the Internet in an hour if you don't back off," Frankie reasons.

Other guys from the football team have joined us, and Gage seems to recognize he's screwed up.

"Look man, I'm not trying to be an asshole. Just looking out for you," Gage takes a step back as he says this, bringing Kayla with him. She's clearly not entirely with it, though, because her eyes are darting around unfocused and she's unsteady on her feet. High or drunk or both, I don't really care.

"Don't," Jace tells him harshly.

"Wes is around here somewhere." Gage gestures in a circle. "I'm sure he can clear up any misunderstanding."

Jace's jaw clenches and I reach for him, unsure how close he is to losing it.

"Frankie, where's the keg?" Jace asks, without taking his eyes off Gage, who keeps backing away until he's swallowed by the crowd.

Before Frankie responds, someone has handed Jace a red solo cup full to the brim, which he immediately chugs. Jace's grasp on my hand is tight and I expect him to lead me away from the party, but instead he leads me to a chair by the fire and pulls me onto his lap.

"What's his problem?" I ask, unable to restrain my curiosity, even if Jace is better off being distracted right now. "Last I knew he was sucking up to you."

Jace rubs his forehead. "It's complicated."

"Secrets aren't cool," I remind him. I'm confused, because most of the ugly in Jace's life comes from his past.

"We will have to get cozier if we want to keep this private." He squeezes my hips and smirks, and some of the tension I'm carrying lifts. He hasn't closed himself off.

"Like this?" I tease, straddling and facing him in front piggy-back style. Now it's just the two of us, our faces inches apart. I don't care if everyone *is* staring. Being Jace Wilder's girlfriend has made me bolder. Stronger. I have to be able to handle the ugly in his life.

As I settle onto his lap, Jace's eyes close and his head tilts back. I inhale sharply, his handsome features striking me as they have millions of times before, and I wonder if it will ever stop. Light flickers from the fire over his sharp jawline and cheekbones, and I study the curve of his lips, tracing my finger along them.

"Wes used to sell to Gage," Jace begins, reminding me why I've positioned myself this way. I remain expressionless. He doesn't know that Wes already told me this. "I didn't like it. I knew Gage was bad news. He's powerful. Did you know his grandfather was a senator?"

I shake my head. No. But I'm not surprised.

"Even though we dealt to a lot of UC guys, we tried to keep a low profile. There wasn't a lot of competition for what we were selling," he pauses and cringes, "so we could afford to be selective about who we distributed to. Anyway, Wes got to know the Sig Beta frat and was convinced Gage was an arrogant prick but would be a good customer. I told him not to, but..." Jace shrugs.

"He did anyway," I finish. Wes is one of the few people who can get away with pissing off Jace without losing his trust or friendship. "So, then what?" I still don't get how this leads to what just happened.

"I'm sure Gage knew or suspected Wes and I worked together or whatever, but Wes can be smart about some shit, at least, and he recently confirmed that Gage was prodding about me but Wes didn't tell him shit."

Jace glances up and Frankie is holding two bottles of beer. Jace grins and takes them. "Thanks man."

"Anytime," Frankie says, and I know they are talking about more than the beer.

Jace offers me one but I shake my head. He puts them both down on the ground and tugs me closer.

"So Gage was a real dick to Wes when he stopped dealing. It was fucking weird. You wouldn't think that anyone would take losing a drug dealer personally, but Gage treated it like a breakup. I don't think the dude even uses himself, but it's like he got off on selling to his frat brothers or something. He also liked being buddies with Wes, I think. Who knows?" Jace's eyes drift from mine, and I can tell that question makes him think about his own reasons for doing what he did.

But Jace never self-contemplates for long. "Anyway, we hadn't heard anything from him until he started kissing my ass when preseason started. I'd actually never officially met the guy before that day in the parking lot. They help everyone on the team with moving, but shit like that has kept happening. He's always inviting me to events he says are exclusive, like I should be honored to get to go. Eventually he wouldn't go away so I had to be a little bit of an asshole," Jace explains, like, *what the hell else was I supposed to do*?

"And he didn't take it well?"

"Apparently not." Jace reaches down to take a long pull from a beer.

"So, no motive in taunting you like he did? Just being immature about getting his feelings hurt because you didn't want to be his friend?" The fact that Gage tried really hard to be Jace's buddy isn't odd. I'm sure most of the fraternity presidents suck up to him. Who wouldn't want Jace Wilder at their parties?

"I don't know. Maybe." Jace frowns, unsure. "He's brought up Wes a few times and I got the feeling he was trying to prod me somehow. This was the first time he's brought you up, but I guess he's been saving that dig for the right moment. Not sure why tonight was it."

"I think he was fucked up. Did you see Kayla? Maybe they were both on something and just acting stupid," I suggest.

"Can't we just hide away and avoid all this drama?" Jace asks.

"What fun would that be?" I joke. We both know that's impossible. And besides, Jace likes being around people, being a leader. It's who he is. He didn't want to go back to the dorm tonight because the people around us rejuvenate him – mostly – and fill him with a sense of purpose. I've accepted that about him, but now he needs to accept it about himself.

Chapter 9

I spend the night in Jace's dorm for the first time. Between classes and morning workouts, I've tried to make it a habit to go home and sleep in my own bed. I don't think Gran would disapprove so that's not an issue. It's that Jace's dorm bed is tiny and it's always noisy. We both need to stay focused and we can't afford a bad night's sleep. But I wake this morning to Jace's hand on my tummy, his body curled around me. I love being the little spoon.

Unfortunately, I'm going to have to make my way to the shared bathrooms. Swinging my legs around and standing up, I grab hold of the dresser as the weight sends shooting pain through my legs, searing my shins in particular. They've ached in the mornings on occasion – okay, maybe every morning for the past few weeks, if I'm honest – but the pain is so intense in this moment I can barely walk. My left one in particular feels like a knife is slicing through it. Sucking in a breath, I sit back down on the bed and begin to gently massage the tendons running along my shins. They finally loosen up enough to allow me to hobble to the bathroom. When I limp back to bed, Jace cracks an eyelid.

"You okay, Pep?" he mumbles from the pillow.

"Yeah," I whisper. "Just achy from the race yesterday. Go back to sleep."

He pulls me in next to him. "Sounds like you could use a massage."

"I bet you could too." I squeeze his biceps playfully.

Jace tenderly rubs his hands over my legs and begins to mold my muscles, gently at first before adding pressure. It's the sweetest way to wake up. If only I hadn't attempted to walk first. Maybe I could have continued to deny what's happening to my shins. Maybe I still will.

By the time we're through with a thorough exchange of massages, we're starved. We'd normally walk to Hal's, our favorite greasy spoon diner, but we're too famished, so we take Jace's Jeep instead. One perk to the athletes' dorm is that they have their own parking lot. Despite the massage loosening up my muscles a bit, my shins still hurt and I probably look like an old granny with arthritis as I hobble to the passenger side.

Jace often has aches and pains after games, but he knows this is unusual for me. I try to brush it off because I can't handle his concern. Denial is the best approach right now. Sometimes people run through these things. My friend who graduated with Jace's class, and my former co-captain, Claire Padilla, once had hip pain early in the season. I don't remember her taking any time off and it just went away on its own. As long as I keep weight training I'll get strong enough to push through this.

Jace takes pity on me and drops me off right in front of the diner before finding parking farther down the street. As he pulls away and I turn to the door, relieved there isn't any sign of people waiting for a table, the front door swings open. When I see it's Ryan Harding, I immediately try to walk normally, praying he didn't catch me limping a moment earlier. I don't want a lecture.

Even worse, he's with his dad, the coach of the UC team, the team I want to be on next year.

"Hi Ryan." I raise my hand in a wave and nod at his dad. "Hi, Mr. Harding."

"Pepper! How are you? And you know it's Mark." He gives me a brief hug, which prompts Ryan to do the same. I haven't seen him since that day outside the gym, right after he broke up with Lisa. And I never did return his phone call.

I've seen Ryan's parents at enough races to feel fairly comfortable with them. But Mark is still the head coach of the team I plan to be on, and I'm always a little nervous around him, wanting to make a good impression. Ryan's younger brother, Kevin, is a freshman at Brockton Public this year, and he's already one of the fastest runners on the varsity team. They congratulate me on the race yesterday and we talk about how Kevin's first high school race went – good, neutral territory. I'm about to ask Ryan about his training when I feel Jace behind me.

This might be the most awkward introduction ever. *"Mr. Harding, this is Jace Wilder, the guy I dumped your son for."* I don't actually say that, but I don't need to. Judging by the way Mark is sizing up Jace, he knows exactly who he is. But they surprise me, greeting each other with handshakes, having met before. I often forget that Ryan and Jace hung out with the same group of friends. It dawns on me that they may have even spent time together this fall at UC. Weird.

After rehashing the football game with Jace, we say our goodbyes. I can feel Ryan watching me as we walk into the diner and I hope he doesn't notice the stiffness in my gait.

We order our usual $4.99 special, with Jace getting coffee and me orange juice.

"You know he's still got it bad for you, right?" Jace asks.

My eyes dart to his. "You heard what Lisa is saying about why they broke up?" I ask, knowing it's not just that. Ryan once told me he could tell Jace felt more than friendship toward me, and I wonder if Jace has the same ability to read other guys. Ryan's certainly more transparent than Jace is about his feelings.

Jace's lips curve into a smile and he laughs softly, shaking his head. He blows on his coffee before taking a sip. "No, Pep. I mean, yeah, I hear what people say about that, but it was obvious before they broke up."

I clench my fork. "Don't treat me like I'm naïve, Jace," I say quietly. "He might have preferred we stay together instead of break up, but he doesn't have it *bad*." I don't want Jace to think I'm oblivious to how my ex-boyfriend feels about me, but I don't want to accept that Ryan is still in love with me because I don't like how that makes me feel. Shitty. There's nothing I can do to make him feel better.

Jace shrugs. "Relax, Pep. I'm not angry about it. I know how the poor guy feels. He was cool about keeping his distance when he was with Lisa. Hopefully he'll keep that up."

"Well, don't worry, that was the first time I've seen him since school started." I'm snappier than necessary. Jace isn't being unreasonable. I'd feel the same way if Jace had an ex-girlfriend. Before me, he never actually had a real girlfriend.

I know my attitude doesn't have much to do with Jace or Ryan though. It's the burning sensation vibrating through my legs that's pissing me off. I will go on a run today, no matter how much it hurts. And that thought makes me so frustrated I actually feel like throwing my fork across the diner. My inner toddler is raging.

When I get home I take twice the prescribed ibuprofen amount and lace up. Dave follows me around in anticipation but I give him a banana – his favorite treat – instead of bringing him with me. I need to be alone, and that includes my canine bestie, for this run, which I anticipate being torturous.

Miraculously, running with severe shin pain isn't much worse than walking with it. At least for the first fifteen minutes...

By the time I get back to Shadow Lane an hour later I'm tempted to crawl up the stairs to our apartment. Instead, I use the railing to help me get to the top. Gran takes one look at me when I stumble into the kitchen and asks me what's wrong.

"Can you run out to the drug store and get three large bags of ice?"

Gran nods solemnly and grabs her keys. She doesn't ask any questions, and I love her for it.

I don't want to say out loud what's happening because then it will be true. Even Gran, who knows next to nothing about training, would tell me to take at least a few days off. But what if I take a few days off and my shins don't get better? What if a few days turns into a few weeks?

Ten minutes later I lower myself into an ice bath. The pain of the ice water hitting my skin and practically stopping my heart is nothing compared to the ache in my chest. Regret. Anger. Confusion. I let the tears stream freely down my face. It's an ugly cry with snot and gasps and I'm sure Gran can hear me out in the hallway. What have I done?

When I finally reflect on it, my shins started to feel tender before school even started. During the summer. I thought it was just an adjustment to ramping up my mileage, and that it would go away as the season went on. I kept telling myself that, even as the mild tenderness became increasingly painful. If I didn't talk about it and didn't think about it, I could pretend it didn't exist. But that can't happen anymore.

A text message from Ryan is waiting for me when I pull myself together enough to leave the bathroom. You were limping. Are you okay? I delete the message.

Gran pokes her head in my room, wringing her hands. She must have heard my meltdown.

"Pepper, why are you hurting yourself like this?" she finally asks.

I close my eyes, hating that question. If only she had tried to tell me to take a break, or that it was okay if I didn't win Nationals, or anything that would allow me to yell back, "You don't understand!"

But she's right. I am hurting myself. And the answer to that question will sound stupid if I say it out loud. *Because I have to. Who am I if not a runner? I need to be someone who matters.* I want to be more than just some girl. I want to make a mark. I don't say any of that.

"I don't know," I say instead.

After a long silence, Gran leaves me alone to bake cookies. The Christmas music comes on as I open my laptop to check my email. Gran always listens to Christmas music when she bakes. It's almost as comforting to hear the music as it is to eat the goodies.

There are several recruitment emails from various schools, but I only click on the one from Oregon. An assistant coach has sent me an itinerary for my trip this weekend. I'll only be there for 24 hours, leaving here on Saturday morning and returning Sunday afternoon, but they've got numerous meals, tours, and... my stomach drops as I take in the scheduled run with the team on Saturday afternoon. What will I do if I can't run?

I slam my computer shut. I still haven't told Jace that I'm leaving this weekend. He has an away game anyway, and I'd rather not bring it up. He'll get all moody like he did last time I brought up Oregon. It's not like I'm actually going to go there, so it might be best to avoid the confrontation all together. No, he'll be pissed when he finds out. And he's bound to find out. Brockton might have nearly 100,000 people living in it, but sometimes it feels like a small town.

A knock at my open door startles me from my contemplation. Gran stands there with a mixing bowl in hand. "You have a visitor."

"Oh?" It can't be Jace, because he would have just waltzed in here.

"It's Ryan," Gran says solemnly. I narrow my eyes at her. Did she call him over here to talk about my... I can't say the "I" word.

"Don't look at me like that. I didn't know he was coming. Maybe he saw you out on the running trail looking like you'd been hit by a truck and decided to come check up on you. Wouldn't be the first time." She hums knowingly as she patters back to the kitchen.

Ryan once found me on the trail in a blizzard, close to collapsing from exhaustion. And now I can barely walk to the kitchen. Thankfully my legs are still slightly numb from the ice bath and I'm able to fake a somewhat normal gait as I make my way to the kitchen table. Ryan is sitting with a glass of milk and oatmeal raisin cookies. Whenever he used to come over Gran would try to "bulk him up" like she does with all of my lean running friends. There's never a shortage of baked goods in our apartment.

He looks up at me as I take a chair on the other side of the table. His light brown hair is shaggy, now long enough to tuck behind his ears. With bright blue eyes and dimples, the longer hair helps detract from the all-American boy look, making him look a little edgier. Like maybe there's a little more to him than we all think.

Jace's words from earlier today ring in my head. Ryan is supposed to keep his distance, especially if he truly does still have feelings for me. But instead, he's sitting at my kitchen table, taking me in like he hasn't seen me in months instead of hours. Oh dear.

He doesn't dance around his reason for being here, and I suppose I'm grateful for that.

"I saw you limping bad on your way into Hal's this morning. And I know you ran an absurdly fast time yesterday, which is awesome. But I'm really worried about you."

I clasp my hands in my lap, hard. Gran places a glass of milk in front of me. I'm glad she's bumbling around the kitchen. That way we're not alone.

"It's not really your place to worry about me, Ryan," I remind him. It's not entirely fair for me to say. If I saw him limping, I'd be worried too.

Ryan's eyes dart away from mine, like I slapped him with my words. "Maybe not, but I can't help it," he admits. "I know you've been at the UC gym lifting three times a week and for all I know, you're running in the morning before afternoon team practices too."

He's right. Not every day, but I run on the mornings I don't lift. I don't bother asking how he knows how often I'm at the gym. There are usually other athletes there, and someone must have mentioned it to him.

"You know you've got four years of college ahead to do double workouts, right?" He means working out twice a day, which is standard fare in college programs. I'd tell him that most high school girls running at my level work out twice a day too, but I get the feeling he just wants to lecture me right now. Which he continues to do for another few minutes before realizing I haven't said a word.

We sit there, studying each other for a moment. "It's my shins," I tell him. "They're a little sore." Gran makes a loud banging noise with a pan, presumably her way of calling me out on my lie. They're more than a little sore. If he goes in our bathroom he'll see the ice still sitting in the tub. Most people wouldn't make themselves an ice bath unless they're seriously hurting.

"You should get an x-ray. I know a really good doctor for running injuries."

He stops short when he notices me cringing at the "I" word.

"It's not an injury. I can still run." More banging in the kitchen.

"Well..." Ryan drawls out the word, like he knows he's walking on thin ice. "Why don't you come in and use the UC pool for a few days? You can do pool running while you let your shins heal."

"Pool running?" I ask skeptically. Sounds like fake running to me.

"You've never done pool running? I do it all the time. It's great when your legs are trashed. I can get you access to the pool and show you."

If I'm going to be able to run with the Oregon team on Saturday, I'm going to have to do something. Maybe this isn't a horrible idea. Technically I'll still be running, just in the water, or whatever. And I can still lift in the mornings.

I agree to meet him tomorrow. He can't meet me until evening because he has his own practice in the afternoon. I'll have to stop by Coach Tom's office to tell him tomorrow. Just sore shins. Nothing major. A few days of pool running is the smart thing to do. Maybe Ryan can get me access to the pool in the mornings too, and I can do it twice a day.

Feeling better that I've got a plan, I respond to the Oregon assistant coach, letting her know I'm looking forward to the trip. Telling Jace about Oregon will be easy compared to telling him about pool running with Ryan.

Chapter 10

The odor of chlorine follows me up the stairs to Jace's dorm late Monday night. Despite a hot shower and thorough hair wash, the scent from the pool lingers on my skin. I've changed into sweats and discussed my plan to spend the night with Gran. She doesn't think it's wise to make it a habit, but she's never been one to impose rules.

My hope is that by surprising him with a sleepover, it'll make up for my pool date...no, not date, *session*...yes, that's better, with Ryan. When we met at the pool at 7:30 tonight, there were only a few lap swimmers and the overhead lights weren't on at full brightness. Running with one other person has a certain intimacy to it – either shared silence or, guaranteed with Zoe or perhaps girls in general, shared chatter. Pool running in bathing suits (I pulled out my Speedo from sophomore year gym class) takes the intimacy thing a little further. Not *that* kind of intimacy, just, you know, a shared sense of purpose or experience or whatever.

I hadn't spoken with Ryan one on one like that in a long time. It felt good to catch up. He told me about his new team, his upcoming meets, how cool it is to finally be able to train with guys who are faster than him. I told him about Zoe, how she's taken on the social scene with an all-consuming energy and she isn't as into running as she used to be. Jenny is our number two runner now, but the rest of the varsity girls aren't very strong, and we probably don't have a shot at winning State again this year. The boys' team might, I told him, with his younger brother already one of the top runners as a freshman.

Pool running turned out to be a good workout, and while I felt my shins – I always feel my shins these days – the pain wasn't excruciating. We imitated the jogging motion in the deep end of the pool until it closed at 8:30.

We kept the conversation away from Lisa, or Jace, or anything too personal. It was a huge relief when Ryan told me he wouldn't be able to meet me for every pool session, but he got permission from the front desk for me – after speaking with Coach Tom – to come in whenever I want. If Ryan was meeting me every day to pool run, I'd practically be spending more time with him than with Jace, which would be quite problematic.

The door to the common area of Jace's four-bedroom dorm suite is wide open, and Frankie sits with their two other roommates on the couch playing a video game. This scenario is typically what's going on when I've left Jace's dorm to head home on other weeknights over the past few weeks. But the four girls perched around the couch in clothing that could be called sleepwear, but would more accurately be labeled lingerie, is a new addition. My jaw drops. What have I walked in on?

The girls stare at me. The boys say hey but keep their eyes glued to the television, engrossed in their game. I straighten my spine, knowing this is no time to show weakness. The girls introduce themselves. I've seen the one named Savannah before, first at the Tavern with Clayton and then at the Theta Kapp party. She's at least six feet tall, which makes her hard to forget.

"We live in the suite below these guys," a girl with pigtail braids tells me. "We're on the soccer team."

"Cool." I say the word and hope I act it. I thought this was a guys-only dorm, but I'm not going to show these girls my ignorance. Must stay strong. "I'm just going to head in there," I say quickly, pointing to Jace's closed door. "Nice to meet you!" I call, already heading that way.

"He's not there, you know," Savannah says, rather bitchily, if I might add. She's incredibly muscular and her aggressive glare gives me chills.

"Yeah, I know." Since when did I lie like this? I totally thought he'd be back from dinner with his mom by now. He doesn't know I'm coming over, so I can't blame him for running late. I continue walking to the door, feigning confidence. But that becomes significantly harder when I turn the doorknob and realize it's locked. I didn't know Jace locked his door because he's always here when I am. Just great.

Taking a deep breath, I turn around and find a table to lean against while I wait. Because there's no way I'm leaving now. If only Frankie would finish his stupid game and save me from these girls already. And I'm pissed at Jace now. Not for being late. But for telling me his dorm was all guys. Ironically, his lie about this makes it a lot easier for me to tell him about Oregon and Ryan, and I let myself gain confidence in that. He kept something from me he thought I wouldn't like, so we're even.

The four soccer girls aren't even pretending not to watch me so I do the same. I'm getting a lot better at this game. I learned quickly that having a tougher skin would be essential to being Jace Wilder's girlfriend. One of the girls is long and lean like me. She has frizzy black hair and soft blue eyes and clearly has a crush on

Frankie. Her curiosity in me doesn't last long before returning to him. The shortest of the four – which isn't saying much because the other three have at least a couple inches on my five foot six height – is perched strategically close to Jace's quietest roommate, Timothy. But Savannah and pigtails haven't stopped eyeing me and I'm struggling to maintain my composure.

What feels like hours but is likely only minutes or even seconds later, Jace walks into the room. He takes in the scene quickly before finding me, his eyes lighting before he breaks into a grin and walks quickly my way. He picks me up and kisses me right in front of everyone and the tension I've been carrying melts away. I can't quite reach around his backpack for a full embrace, but after a you-don't-matter-to-me wave at the girls (the guys grunt hello, still oblivious to anything but the TV), Jace unlocks his door and we're alone.

"This is a nice surprise." He holds my hips and takes me in from head to toe. "You smell like the pool." He raises a dark eyebrow.

"I went pool running today to let my legs recover from Saturday's race."

"Oh?" Jace knows there's more to it and he's waiting patiently for me to explain. This isn't our normal routine, and the concern in his gaze fills me with both love and guilt. He thinks I'm here because I need him to talk about what's up with my training, but that's only a small reason I'm here. I do need him. Always. But I also need to confess.

Instead, I take the cowardly route, and start with an accusation.

"Those girls told me they live downstairs. You told me this wasn't a co-ed dorm."

"I wish it wasn't," Jace says with annoyance. "Those girls are always dropping in. I thought I'd heard it was guys only in our dorm, but I was wrong. The guys and girls are on different floors instead of intermingled on the same floor like the other dorms. That's the only difference."

"Why didn't you say something? Don't you think that's something I'd want to know?"

Jace frowns at me, his hands still on my hips. "Not really. I didn't think it was a big deal. I'm pretty much never here, unless I'm sleeping or with you. I usually study at the public library in my mom's office. You can't actually get any work done at the college libraries. People everywhere." Annie is a librarian at the Brockton Public Library.

"Or here, if those girls are always around," I add. "Do they come over every night?" They looked pretty comfortable, and I'm not usually here this late at night.

"Yeah, the soccer and basketball girls live here and they stop by a lot, but it's just to hang out with the other guys. I've gotten a reputation as never being around or having my door closed. There's no privacy around here, Pep, it sucks."

His hands drop lower and he pulls me to him, and I realize he doesn't even feel guilty for keeping this from me. And he's right, it shouldn't be a big deal. But it feels like one. Maybe if I approach my news with the same attitude he did...

"So I also have something-you-probably-won't-like-but-isn't-a-big-deal to tell you."

Jace's hands drop now. "Okay, now this sounds like a big deal."

"I'm going to Oregon this weekend," I blurt.

"Okay," Jace replies, a question in his voice, like, is that all? He knows me too well.

"Yeah, you know, I just really want to see the school and learn about the program a little. For the experience, not because I really want to go there."

"Yeah, okay," he says again, nodding.

"Really? It's okay?"

"I'm not going to give you a hard time for visiting other schools, Pep. I get it. Yeah, I'm probably going to worry about you loving it so much somewhere else you want to go there instead, but if that happens, we'd figure it out."

"What?!" Jace would be okay with me leaving the state? We'd never see each other. Like, *never*. We'd definitely break up then, wouldn't we? And he's acting like it's no big deal.

Jace sighs, rubbing his messy dark hair and face. "I mean, I'm not going to be a controlling boyfriend. I have controlling tendencies and I've gotta do my best to rein them in."

"Where is Jace Wilder and what have you done with him?" Jace is never self-reflective like this, and if he is, he never shares those thoughts with me.

Jace smiles sheepishly. "My mom and I have been having some good talks. She's giving me a lot of good advice."

Whoa. I had no idea. This is what Jace has always wanted. A mother-son relationship. When she moved here months ago, he sought her approval and went out of his way to spend time with her. But he always kept a barrier there, which frankly I was happy about, because I didn't want him to get hurt if she left again.

I'm strangely a little jealous that he's been having deep conversations with his mother. Not so much that they aren't with me – some conversations aren't meant to be between boyfriend and girlfriend – but that he has a mom and I don't. Mine died when I was so young I don't even remember her, besides what Gran tells me. I love Gran and she's been there for me, but she's not my mom. Jace has two real parents now, and a brother. And who do I have?

"Hey, relax." Jace takes my hands. "I hear it rains all the time in Oregon. You'll probably hate it."

I guess he can't always read my mind. He thinks I'm worried about where I'll go to college.

"And also, it was Ryan who got me in to the pool today and showed me how to pool run."

That gets the reaction I predicted. The familiar jaw clenching and green eyes narrowing.

"And I'm not sure what Annie would advise, but I get it if this pisses you off. He should be keeping his distance, you're right. And that's true no matter how he feels or doesn't feel. But, well, I did need to do something about the pain in my legs, and this was a good idea."

"Yeah, I really don't fucking like it," Jace says honestly.

"Look, he was just trying to help, and he won't be joining me again. I have access to the pool on my own now and I know what I'm doing."

"You mean this wasn't a one-time thing?" Jace's grip on my hips is becoming uncomfortably tight, but I don't say anything.

"Well, with him it was, but I need to pool run all week so my legs are recovered enough to run with the Oregon team this weekend."

"What's going on with your legs anyway, Pep? I'm starting to worry here. Do you need to see a doctor?"

And I lie, again, saying it's nothing serious, just a little soreness. I can practically hear Gran banging pans in the kitchen.

"Look, I know I'm biased here, but I have to say this. Sometimes I think the good guy thing Ryan has going on is just an act."

"What?" Sure, Jace has a right to be wary of my ex-boyfriend who remains on the peripheries of my life because of all we've got in common, but this comment is just petty. And Jace has never been petty before.

"Just, maybe don't trust his intentions too blindly."

Now I'm not only feeling slightly insulted, but I'm put in the awkward position of feeling compelled to defend my ex-boyfriend in front of my current boyfriend.

"Can we talk about something else?" I ask instead.

Jace pulls me onto his bed and we lie there, his hand slipping easily under my clothes and resting on my lower back.

"Wes came to dinner tonight with Annie."

"Yeah?" I grasp onto this subject change.

"Yeah, they've interacted a couple times but never really like, intentionally, you know? And he *is* my brother, even if through weird circumstances that sort of required dad cheating on Annie, but yeah, it seemed right she should get to know him a little. Maybe you can come to our next dinner?"

"I'd like that." My feelings toward his mom have warmed significantly since she first arrived, which means they are still only lukewarm. She might have good intentions but she left her son once before, and as Jace would say, I'm not going to trust so blindly. I'd give him the same advice he gave me about Ryan, but telling someone who already doesn't trust easily not to trust his own mother seems like a really bad idea.

"I wish you'd spend the night again. It wasn't so bad sharing such a small bed the other night, was it?"

"You're in luck," I whisper in his ear. "I'm yours until 8:05 first period."

And with that, my sweatpants are gone and thrown against the door, the rest of the world forgotten.

Chapter 11

I don't look forward to lunch anymore. Sure, Gran still packs me an excellent lunch box every day, but now that my friends have merged with the popular people (or have we become those people? I don't even know), it's gossip central. And a lot of it has to do with me. Indirectly, at least. First I was the reason Ryan and Lisa broke up, and now that that's old news, people are talking about how Jace Wilder is not the party guy people thought he'd be at UC, and it's my fault.

"I hear Jace like, stays in his room or is never around. He's like a hermit or something now that he's in college!" Dana exclaims before biting into her apple. I think that's what she eats for lunch every day. And that's it.

"Who told you that?" Diego, the guy who finally got to be first-string quarterback when Jace graduated, asks.

"Oh, everyone knows it. But you know, like..." and Dana proceeds to list off a dozen of her UC friends. It's like she paid Diego to ask that question so she could show how popular she is with the college crowd.

The thing is, they all expect me to weigh in. This is a realistic expectation. But true friends wouldn't gossip about your boyfriend in front of you. At least they don't say what I know the rumors are saying – that it's because of me Jace is no fun. Do they ever think that maybe he's focused on football too? Because that's the main reason both of us are buckling down. We have high expectations placed on us, and we want to reach our goals. On top of that, we have to go to classes and do homework. Neither of us are in the running for academic excellence, but we don't want to fail out either.

Thankfully, Zoe gets this, and she tactfully steers the topic away to other gossip – namely, a party they all went to on Saturday night and can you believe that Justin and Delilah broke up after two years together?

"Speaking of Saturday night," Tina chimes in, "Pepper, I heard you were at a party on campus with Jace?"

All eyes turn to me.

"See? Jace isn't a hermit after all." I try not to sound bitchy about it, but it's hard. Thank you Tina, for contradicting your BFF.

"Didn't he, like, beat up the president of Sig Beta because he said you were cheating on him with Wesley Jamison?" Tina is relentless.

"No, that's not what happened." I don't want to take the bait, but I know that if I don't give her *something*, she'll probably take my silence as an admission I'm cheating on Jace, or worse. "The president was being an asshole." That gets their attention. I hardly ever curse. "He knows Jace and I are friends with Wes and made some stupid comment about it, I don't even remember, and Jace got annoyed but that's about it. It wasn't a big deal." I shrug, downplaying the event that was indeed very close to turning into a fistfight, and did actually involve some harsh insinuations about me and Wes.

"So... you and Wesley?" Dana asks.

"Are you serious?" I'm not the meek girl I used to be. I won't put up with someone asking, in front of my friends, and what I realize is half the lunchroom, if I'm cheating on my boyfriend. "That probably doesn't even deserve a response but no, of course not."

I grab the rest of my lunch and stand up to leave. Zoe follows me, and I'm thankful for her camaraderie.

"I'm sorry," she says beside me when we finally leave the cafeteria and reach the empty hallway. We're not supposed to be roaming the corridors during lunch period, but whatever.

"It's not your fault."

"It kind of is. I mean, I started hanging out with them."

"Yeah, but so did Rollie and Omar, and I get it. They go to all the parties and have tons of fun. But they suck at having a normal conversation without being total bitches."

"Whoa, Pepper," Zoe says laughing, not used to my vengeful comments.

I shrug. "Just saying. And they'd be saying worse about me if I wasn't there, so maybe I can curb it with my presence."

"You might actually be enhancing the gossip. They think they know you now which gives them free rein to talk about you."

I glare at her. "Maybe you *should* be apologizing then."

"I can break up with them. I don't think anyone's feelings would be hurt," she offers.

"Nah, I'd rather avoid the drama of that going down. By the way… I haven't heard much about Charlie."

We've arrived at the back doors to the athletic fields and we tacitly agree to break more school rules by opening them and wandering outside.

"Actually, we kind of broke up," she tells me without much emotion.

I stop walking. "What? Why? When?"

"Chill, chill," she says, laughing. "You know it was never super serious with us. I mean, yeah, I love Charlie and we'll always be friends, but we're not getting married. It's just hard when he's off at college a couple hours away and we've both got a lot of stuff going on. It was kind of mutual but I guess I brought it up first. It just happened yesterday."

This news makes me incredibly sad. Which is odd, because Zoe doesn't even seem fazed. But if they only lasted a few weeks once college started, how can Jace and I make it? I know we're different, but it's not like we've talked about marriage either. Zoe and Charlie were in love. She still loves him. She lost her virginity to him. And even if Jace and I stay together until I go to UC too, that's no guarantee of anything either. Ryan and Lisa broke up when college started. Sometimes, no matter how good it's going, I can't get rid of this feeling that the odds are against us.

***

I took five full days off from running and my shins still hurt when I ran with the Oregon team. My left one in particular shot acute pain through my body with each step. The girls were all chatting my ears off about the school, which helped distract me a bit, but it was a huge relief when we finished. And then I had to pretend to walk normally the rest of the day.

The weirdest thing was learning that at least a third of the team was injured with something or other. And it seemed like everyone on the team was either in recovery or nursing an old injury. I didn't know what to make of this, and as I hop on Zoe's bike back in Brockton on Sunday afternoon, I'm still not sure what to make of my painful shins. Is this something all runners go through and just push through? Or is taking a break part of being a serious runner too? I'm too afraid to admit that I might have the "I" word.

I ride Zoe's bike to the UC track, unable to run there like I normally would. Just the thought of running makes me feel like puking. My shins feel broken. Slowly and using the railing, I make my way to the top of the stadium stairs, where I have a view of the foothills overlooking the track. It's empty and the only sound is birds chirping.

It was fun going on a plane again for only my second time, and meeting girls who are as hardcore about running as I am, but it feels so right sitting on these stadium steps. Even with the "I" word haunting me, I know that this track in front of me is where I belong. I can see myself doing 400 repeats with my future teammates, and racing to cheering fans – Jace included. He'll be off from football in the spring and he'll come to my meets.

Decision made – or reinforced, more accurately - I check in to see if Jace is around, but he's lifting weights with his team, so I decide to head to the pool. My phone beeps as I'm hopping back on Zoe's bike.

Ryan: how was Oregon? Want 2 pool run tonight? No practice today 4 me.

Me: Oregon was fun. Going to pool now.

I figure it's too last-minute for him, and I'd rather he didn't join me. It's not that I agree with Jace that Ryan is only putting on a good guy act, but having a friendship with Ryan isn't worth hurting Jace. Sure, Ryan's great at giving running advice, and he's easy to talk to, but I don't need him like I need Jace. I can live without Ryan in my life if it means keeping Jace and me on solid terms.

Unfortunately, five minutes into my pool run there's a loud splash in front of me as I nearly crash into a tan body. Ryan's grinning at me with those adorable dimples and hair that's now long enough to give him a surfer-boy vibe. For just a moment the thought crosses my mind that there might be some mischief underneath that sweet appearance after all.

"I hear you've been in here every day, sometimes twice a day," he says in a mock-scolding tone. Okay, knowing my lifting routine didn't seem that out of the ordinary, but now I'm wondering if he's keeping tabs on me.

Ryan puts his hands up in an innocent gesture as he treads water. "Relax, the front desk girl told me. She's the one who talked to Coach Tom about it."

"Right. Whatever." Why am I suddenly annoyed with him? Did Jace plant a seed for this purpose? Should I be annoyed with Jace instead? This is too confusing.

"So what'd you think of OU?" He starts pool jogging beside me.

"It was cool, I guess." But I don't want to talk about me, especially about an important topic that I haven't even discussed with my boyfriend yet. "You had your first college race yesterday, right?"

Ryan takes the hint. "Oh yeah, it was just like an unofficial scrimmage thing. You'd be surprised how many people get injured early in the season and end up redshirting. This meet lets people race unofficially so they can still decide to redshirt if they get injured or whatever." I've always known that redshirting was pretty commonplace for football players. They often take freshman year off from college competition, which allows them to get bigger and stronger, but requires being in college for five years. I didn't know it was common for runners, and apparently not to get bigger or stronger but because of that dreaded word.

"You're not planning on redshirting, are you?"

"No, I've been feeling great. I'm only pool running with you, Pepper, because, well, to spend time with you."

I turn sharply and give him a look.

"Is that not okay?" he asks innocently, and I scrutinize him, wondering if it's *too* innocent.

"Probably not, actually," I say truthfully. "You're my ex-boyfriend and I have a boyfriend. We should keep our space." I don't want to hurt his feelings, but he's got to see that this isn't appropriate.

"Yeah, yeah, you're right." Ryan nods quickly. "I'm sorry, Pepper."

When we reach the other end of the pool he climbs out without another word, leaving me feeling like a jerk. He's just trying to help me out, after all. Right? I study his dejected and embarrassed expression as he walks to the locker room in his swimming shorts. I'm not sure what to think anymore. It was a lot easier when Ryan was just straightforward and one-dimensional.

Two hours later I've managed to clean off most of the chlorine and I've even dressed up for dinner with Jace at my favorite Mexican restaurant. It's not quite warm enough for a dress but I wear one anyway, knowing this may be my last opportunity before the weather changes.

Jace is waiting for me in front of the restaurant with flowers when I arrive on Zoe's bike, which I think I might just keep for good, and I wonder if this is an important date I've forgotten. He takes in my flowy dress and cowboy boots and smiles. "Come here," he tells me, and I easily comply.

"Is there an occasion I'm forgetting?" I ask.

"No, but we haven't had a real date in a while and I thought it'd be nice."

"When did you become so romantic?" I tease, leaning on my toes to kiss him on the cheek.

"I think you know when," he says with a wink as he leads me inside.

The restaurant is family-owned, and apparently the owners are UC football fans because they bring us a bottle of red wine on the house. Jace glances at me in question, and I shrug, thinking a glass of wine might not be so bad. I've never had red, and I might not like it, but it feels very sophisticated and adult-like. We're finishing a chocolate torte and trying to decide which night this week we can have a sleepover when a large group of college guys takes the table near our booth.

Jace glances at them out of the corner of his eye and when his jaw clenches I follow his gaze. I recognize the

Sig Beta guys and start to feel a wave of relief when I don't see Gage Fitzgerald, but my relief is short-lived when he joins the group – at the head of the table, which places him right next to us – a moment later. Just our luck.

Jace reaches for his wallet to leave some bills without awaiting the check. I take one last sip of wine (okay, more like gulp) and grab my jacket and purse. Jace takes my hand and pulls me out of the booth but Gage spots us before we can avoid him.

"Oh, hey guys!" he greets us like old friends. So obnoxious. "Yeah, Pepper, you must have been really hungry after that swim earlier."

My head whips to Gage at that comment but Jace tugs me along, and I'm proud of him for avoiding confrontation; a year ago that would not have been the case. But the chairs are all pulled out and we can't get through easily.

Gage keeps talking in that cocky voice of his. "You spend a lot of time in bathing suits with other guys. You know we've got a hot tub at Sig Beta that doesn't require bathing suits, right? Can't guarantee I'll take you out to dinner afterward like Wilder, here, though."

Before I can even process the insult, Jace has Gage by the collar against the wall and his chair is knocked over. Gage must have been expecting a reaction, but his face has gone white with the pressure Jace is putting on him. I can't hear what Jace is saying, and before any of the frat brothers can intervene, Jace has dropped Gage, who slumps to the floor before quickly straightening himself up. Jace hurries me out of the restaurant, mumbling a "sorry" to our waiter, who is standing mouth agape when we pass him.

We drive in silence and it takes me a moment to realize we're heading toward Shadow Lane instead of the dorms.

"Are you mad at me?" I ask.

He's gripping the steering wheel with both hands. "I don't know yet," he says through a clenched jaw. "I don't fucking like having shit thrown at me that I don't even know about. What the hell was he talking about this time?"

This time. Like maybe Gage is right and I *am* spending too much time in bathing suits with other guys.

"Ryan showed up at the pool while I was pool running today." Before I can elaborate, Jace interrupts me.

"Pep, we talked about this. Did he know you were going? Did you invite him?" *Do you still have feelings for him?* is the question he's really asking.

I shake my head rapidly. "No, no. I mean, he texted me and I told him I was going pool running but I didn't invite him. Here, I'll show you the text." And I do at the next stop light. He reads them quickly before handing me back the phone, not showing any reaction.

"But most importantly I told Ryan to keep his distance and he left like two minutes after he got there. I think I actually hurt his feelings," I say, hoping Jace will realize it wasn't easy for me to do.

Jace remains silent until he pulls in front of my house. I'm disappointed. We haven't spent much time together since my Monday night sleepover nearly a week ago. I don't know what else to say. I try, "I'm sorry."

He finally turns to look at me and I wait, hoping for a kiss, a smile, a shrug. Anything to indicate we're good. "I'm just feeling a lot of anger right now, Pep," he admits. "I think it's mostly directed at Gage and maybe some at Ryan, but I don't want to direct it at you and regret it later." This mature Jace, who thinks through what he's feeling and articulates his emotions, is still so very new to me. I'm impressed.

"I get it," I say quietly. "But can I at least have a kiss?" I say with what I hope is a coy smile.

He doesn't hesitate. His lips connect with mine for a wonderful minute before he pulls away gently. "I'm going to check in with my dad, okay? We'll touch base later."

Reluctantly, I head back inside. When someone who is nearly a complete stranger to both of us is determined to get between Jace and me, it seems like we'll never catch a break. Will Jace Wilder always attract people who want to challenge him? If he remains on top, the answer is yes. And given that he's been "a hermit" recently and still can't avoid hordes of attention, I fear we will never be free from it. The only choice we have is to stay strong and fight it.

Chapter 12

Burning pain sears along my shins as I surge ahead of Rollie and Omar on the second of four roughly one-mile intervals. It's a workout we do every other Monday. The path is marked off by cones but most of us on varsity don't need the direction, as we've done this workout so many times before. It starts out up a hill, takes a short loop in the woods and ends with a lap around the baseball field. The girls' team, except for me, does it three times with four minutes' rest between. I do the loop four times with the boys' team.

I'm still able to run as fast as ever but the lightning bolts shooting along my left shin make it a very unpleasant experience. Apparently taking a week off to pool run did not fix the problem. When I surge around the baseball dugout I'm breathing like I'm winded, but it's not because I'm at my threshold... at least not my endurance threshold. My pain threshold is definitely being tested though, and it's not the kind of pain I can just push through like I normally would. My left shin has a life of its own and it's making every step brutal.

Coach Tom approaches me when I finish the lap as I start my watch for the rest interval. "You need to call it quits for the day, Pepper."

And it's like he's twisted a knife in my gut. Those are the words I have been dreading from him. The pain is almost as bad as my shins. *Almost.* Which is why I don't protest. He's right. I can't keep this up. And Coach Tom wouldn't let me anyway. He knows my running stride better than anyone, and he must be able to tell by watching me that I'm hurting.

I nod in acquiescence but I'm unable to speak through the lump in my throat.

"Head on over to the trainers for some ice. We're going to get you in to see a doctor tomorrow."

The knife twists again. Trainers. Ice. Doctors. *Call it quits.* I feel like I might be sick all over the grass as I walk away, refusing to make eye contact with my teammates.

The training room is full of sweaty bodies. I've only been in here once or twice before and it was just to grab some tape or a water bottle or something. A young woman spots me and introduces herself as Jessie. She seems to know who I am already as she sets me up at a table and begins touching my legs. When she presses gently on my left shin and asks if it's tender to the touch, my eyes water with discomfort and I nod silently. She repeats the exercise on other parts of my lower leg and then the other leg, using only a brush of pressure to touch the muscles. But it still hurts.

Eventually she hooks me into something she calls E-stim – electrical muscle stimulation. The name of the machine alone almost sends me into a panic attack. It sends a strange tingling feeling through my lower legs. The sensation is like ants crawling around in my muscles. It doesn't make the pain go away, but it's a distraction, I guess.

I keep my eyes glued to the television. It's on ESPN but I'm not really processing anything. I'm well aware that the noise level decreased significantly when people noticed I was in here with... gulp... an *injury*. Along with Clayton Dennison, Ryan Harding and Jace Wilder, I'm one of the most decorated Brockton Public athletes. I'm the only girl to win Nationals in any sport, and with

Ryan winning for the boys in the very same year, we attracted a lot of attention to Brockton Public. A news station even came and filmed us at school one time. Out of the corner of my eye I see someone typing on their phone, and I have a feeling news that I'm here and hooked into an E-stim machine will spread quickly.

Jessie is huddled with a more senior trainer – Bob, I think his name is. They glance at me, ignoring the dozen other athletes who might need their attention, and I can't help the weary sigh that escapes.

After what feels like days, Coach Tom shows up, nods at the trainers, and settles himself on the stool next to the table I'm perched on.

"So, are you going to tell me what's going on?" he asks.

I point at the wires on my shins. "They hurt."

"I see that. How long?"

"A while," I admit.

"Pepper, how long have your shins hurt?" he asks again.

"Probably August." It's October now. "Before school started." It's bad. Saying it aloud, I feel like a total idiot. Why did I ignore this for not days, not weeks, but months?

The two trainers join us. Bob forgoes any pleasantries, announcing, "Looks like you've done a number on those shins of yours, Ms. Jones. You may have a stress fracture in the left one. We can't know for sure without x-rays, but it sure sounds like it."

Twist that knife again, Bob, pull it out, stab it back in. I must be white as a sheet because Coach puts his hand on my forehead. "Grab us a cold washcloth, Bob, will you?"

"What does that mean? When can I run again?" I ask, letting Jessie place the cold towel on my forehead.

"You'll need to go in for x-rays first thing tomorrow. Dr. Kennedy is an orthopedic specialist who frequently works with our athletes, but I don't think you've seen her before." Bob's voice vibrates in my ear, but I know he's not speaking very loudly.

A stress fracture. In October of my senior year. I may not get a scholarship to UC after all. What happens if I don't get a scholarship? I'll have to go somewhere that gives me one, and it won't be in Brockton. October won't leave me enough time to recover and compete in the qualifying meets for Nationals. I'll have to take weeks, maybe even months off.

"Calm down, Pepper," Coach Tom says and it sounds like he's far away, though I know he's right next to me. "It's going to be okay. This is a common running injury that we can work through and bounce back from. You're going to be right back at it before you know it."

But, it's my senior cross season, Coach, I want to yell. I'm supposed to win Nationals, and instead, I'll be hobbling around, unable to run at all.

I nod at their questions about booking me a doctor's appointment tomorrow morning. They will get me out of class somehow. It doesn't feel real as I hobble back to Zoe's bike, which I've decided to keep until she pries it out of my hands. I've never had my own car and I love the freedom of being able to get around town without one. Especially now that I can't just run everywhere I want. But there's a familiar Escalade waiting in the nearly-empty parking lot, and Wesley Jamison hops down from the driver's seat.

"Need a ride?" he calls.

"What are you doing here?"

He catches up to me and takes my bike once I've unlocked it from the rack. I let him roll it to his car.

"Word spreads fast when Pepper Jones splits in the middle of a workout to go to the trainers," he says as an answer.

"Okaaay." I'll never get used to the minor-celebrity status my running accomplishments have elevated me to in Brockton. "But that doesn't explain why you're here," I remind him.

"Jace heard, couldn't come because he was still at practice, and got in touch with me. He thought you might try riding home on Zoe's bike," Wes says pointedly as he hauls her bike into his trunk.

I roll my eyes. "I can still ride a bike."

"Whatever, Pep, you know you'd rather ride with me."

His help into the passenger seat is appreciated, as it's dawning on me just how much of an invalid I have become. Beating the boys in the first two laps at practice today sent me over the edge. I simply cannot deny that I'm injured. Somehow, though, I'm keeping a safe distance from the reality of it, maintaining the fuzzy haze of shock I experienced in the training room. It's like I'm partially in a dream, living in someone else's body. That's Wes right there, turning up the radio, but I'm detached from really being in this car with him.

He takes me back to the apartment and talks to Gran in the kitchen while I shower. When we sit down for dinner, a chicken and green bean casserole that I can barely pick at, Gran tells me she'll drive me to the appointment tomorrow. Wes has told her already, or maybe Coach called, because I don't remember telling anyone about the doctor appointment. I'm thankful she knows, either way, because I'm not sure I can say it aloud yet.

It dawns on me that Wes hasn't joined us for a family dinner in a long time. I shake my head, realizing I haven't seen him at all since the swimming outing. That's really strange. He spilled his guts to me, showed up on a whim to hang out, and then disappeared. I suppose I've been busy, and Jace has too, and we usually all hang out together. It's not like when they were in high school anymore, when we all showed up to the same parties most weekends.

But didn't Gage say Wes was at that party last weekend? I'm lost in my own thoughts, partially about what Wes might have been up to, but mostly with painful anticipation of the news I will receive tomorrow. Even sitting at the table, the soreness in my legs resonates through me, a constant reminder of my failure.

I haven't paid attention to a word Wes and Gran are saying when Jace busts open the door like he's on a mission. He takes one look at me and strides forward, kneeling by my chair. I imagine I look a little lost right now, even sitting at home eating dinner like I do nearly every night. With my running goals stripped from me, I'm not sure what my purpose is anymore.

"Hey," he says quietly. "We're going out tonight, okay? To a concert. It'll be fun and you can be out late since you're skipping morning classes."

How does everyone know about the doctor appointment already?

"The appointment's at nine, right Buns?" Jace asks Gran.

"Yup. Take this girl out. Have some fun!"

I'm not about to protest. Wallowing in my thoughts alone in my room is the last thing I want to do right now.

Wes and Jace are, apparently, on a mission to save me from misery. First we drive to Clyde's Creamery and they essentially force-feed me a chocolate mint ice cream cone. It's my favorite, but I can't finish. My emotions are so volatile I'm not sure when they'll erupt and for that reason, I'm queasy.

A local band is playing at Clifford's, a theater on Main Street that's been around forever. I'm still only seventeen and officially, you're supposed to be eighteen to go to a show at Clifford's, but everyone knows that as long as you look older than twelve, no one will care.

Wes and Jace don't know much about the band, only that the drummer is supposed to be awesome, and Wes thinks he remembers there's a girl who sometimes plays the piano with them who's "smoking" – but he's not talking about her musical talent.

The theater is dark and smoky – not from cigarettes, but a cloud of marijuana. I've never smoked myself, but I'm

119

familiar with its sweet, earthy scent. It's not too packed, but it's only the opening band up there.

I gesture to the ledge along the side of the wall, hoping to get off my legs. Jace lifts me up before jumping up after me. Wes is already lost in the crowd, doing his social butterfly thing.

"I'm worried about him," Jace tells me. The music is loud, but he has his head right next to mine so I can hear.

"Yeah? I haven't seen him in a while. Have you?" I ask.

"Not much. A couple of times we've watched games together at Dad's house, but he knows I've been busy with football, classes, and you of course," he says with a nudge.

"What makes you worry?"

"I've heard he's been at a lot of UC parties."

"That's not really surprising, is it?"

"I get a feeling he's getting into the drug scene again. People act a little sketchy when his name comes up and I'm around."

I'm not exactly sure what that means, but I guess if people knew Jace used to deal drugs with Wes, and that they both got out of it, but now Wes was back in... well, it would be easy to infer that Jace wouldn't be happy about it. People don't know the two of them are brothers, but they do know that they're close.

"Did he get a job?" I ask.

"Nope. That's another reason I'm worried. What the hell is he doing with his time? My dad asked him if he wanted to work a construction job with him, and he said he'd think about it. I don't know what he has to think about."

I can't help but wonder if Wes thinks he's too good for construction work, which is what Jim has done his whole life. Wes's other dad would flip if Wes deferred Princeton for a construction job in Brockton. But what if Wes is doing something illegal instead?

Chapter 13

I find Wes in the smoky room. He's standing next to two girls in tight tank tops and ripped jeans. The three of them are swaying to the music. A guy taps Wes on the shoulder, says something in his ear, and Wes shakes his head. I continue watching him, trying to pinpoint anything suspicious, until the opening band starts packing up and the headliner for the night sets up.

Jace hops down to grab us some drinks – sodas, not beers – but I stay put, happy to guard our spot if it means staying off my legs. My eyes lock on Wes again, and he's taking one of the ripped-jeans girls out a side exit. Well, random hookups are better than the alternative, I suppose. Now that I know a little bit about the underlying pain behind his fleeting hookups, though, I continue to worry for him.

A hand tugs my ankle and I glance up to find Clayton Dennison standing far too close to me, his height bringing his eyes right to my chest-level. Two girls and another guy with a UC baseball cap stand nearby. One of the girls I recognize as Savannah, a soccer player who lives in Jace's dorm. She was the one who gave me chills. Mostly because she's an amazon. Taller than most of the guys in the theater, with broad shoulders and long thick hair that flows nearly to her waist. She's got high cheekbones and striking features and if it wasn't for her muscle mass, she could walk the runway.

She's sizing me up again, in that way that sends goose bumps down my spine. This one has that evil Madeline Brescoll aura about her. Madeline has headed off to college somewhere on the east coast, and while I figured I'd always have some bitchy girls to shake off as long as

I remained with Jace Wilder, I never thought I'd face one as vicious as Madeline. But something about amazon-girl sets me on edge.

"I heard you broke a record last weekend. Congrats," Clayton says, keeping my ankles in his hands. I could kick them off, but that might be a bit dramatic.

"Thanks." He notices me looking at amazon-girl and apparently doesn't interpret the glances as wariness, because he gestures her over.

"Savannah, this is Pepper Jones. Brockton Public Running Phenomenon," he quotes from a newspaper headline from last cross season. He must not recall that he introduced us already at the Tavern weeks ago.

"Yeah, I know who she is, Clay," Savannah says, chewing her gum loudly.

"Savannah's a sophomore. She's a striker on the soccer team. Lead scorer this season, right?" he asks.

She shrugs, but her fake-nonchalance doesn't fool me. She likes that Clayton Dennison knows her stats. After all, if she can't have Jace Wilder, Clayton is the next best in the male athlete hierarchy. I've heard there's a dude on the field side of the track and field team who was runner-up at Nationals in the shot put last year, but if his picture on the homepage of the team website is accurate, he's probably 300 pounds and very scary looking. So yeah, Clayton might not have the accolades in his sport that the shot put guy has, but he's got the classic good looks to make him a hot commodity. Plus, let's be honest, a lot more people show up to watch baseball games than shot put.

Clayton introduces the other guy and girl, and when he still hasn't released my ankles (actually, his hands have crept up to my calves now) I muster my courage to stand up to the hot shot baseball player.

"Clayton, can you stop touching my legs, please?" My voice is loud and clear, and I've made an effort to sound as genuine as possible. I'm convinced my request embarrasses him in front of his friends, but he just chuckles.

"I just thought you might have some magic in those legs that I could use on the field," he teases, leaning uncomfortably close.

Savannah glares at me before glancing over her shoulder. Her eyes light up when she sees someone she recognizes and she walks away.

"There's nothing magical about me, Clayton," I tell him, keeping an eye on Savannah. When I see who she's approached, I'm tempted to jump right on down, but there's a chance my shins will literally shatter if I do that. Instead, I try to make eye contact with Jace, who is holding a soda in each hand.

He tries to side-step Savannah, but she blocks him against the wall with those absurdly muscular hips. Jace's eyes dart to mine and when he sees who is hovering by me, I hope he finds humor in the situation. But instead, the familiar jaw clench reveals only frustration. He looks so sexy when he's angry.

Clayton continues to position himself inappropriately by my legs, and the guy and girl he was with have drifted closer to the stage, farther from us. Did these two plan this ambush or something? What the heck is going on?

"You know, Pepper Jones, I was pretty upset when you shot me down for prom back in high school. Why'd you do that?"

"Why'd you ask me?" I retort. We both know why he asked.

He pulls his head back in surprise. "Oh come on, you're just fishing for compliments. Isn't it obvious why I asked?"

I raise my eyebrows but remain silent.

"Uh, because you're a cool girl. Not wrapped up in any drama. Or, at least, you weren't back then," he says with a smirk. "You're a kickass runner, which makes you even hotter than most girls."

I can't help my eye roll. "You'd never even spoken to me before. You didn't know anything about me. And I was a freshman. Just admit that you were trying to get under Jace's skin. You were then and you are now."

Instead of arguing with me or getting angry, Clayton flashes a lopsided grin, making him look a little crazy. He opens his mouth and begins to speak, but Jace is suddenly between us, and I no longer feel suffocated by Clayton's body inching inappropriately closer to me.

"Hey, Dennison," Jace casually greets him after placing himself between us. I don't think I've ever witnessed Jace Wilder being fake with someone before, so this is a first. "Wesley told me he's been running into you a lot lately."

My brows furrow in confusion. What's he talking about?

Clayton straightens to his full height. The freshman quarterback and junior pitcher both tower over everyone else in the theater. Savannah holds her own, having returned with Jace. She doesn't know their history, but her wide eyes dart between the two of them, sensing the tension.

"Yeah, Wes has a lot of time on his hands these days and he wants to stay in shape. He joins us in some of the team's unofficial lifting sessions," Clayton responds after a moment's hesitation.

"Right, well, good luck with MLB scouts, man." Jace hands me our drinks and pats Clayton on the shoulder, hard, judging by Clayton's wince, before propelling himself up to the ledge in one swift athletic move and kissing me on the top of my head.

As Clayton and Savannah make their way back to their friends I turn to Jace. "Jiggawhat?" I give him my one-word question, which really means, please explain what the heck just happened?

Jace grins, but it's tinted with regret. "Well, my suspicion about Wes was right, I guess."

"What was that? Clayton Dennison can't be a drug addict, Jace. You mean you think he deals with Wes or something?" I just don't understand how an athlete at Clayton's level can get away with a recreational drug habit. Not only would it make training impossible, but Division I athletes get tested, don't they?

"I think Wes is just dealing steroids. Still bad, but it doesn't involve him with the Denver gang or Wolfe's crowd, at least." Just hearing that name sends shivers up my spine. Wolfe was angry that Jace didn't help him make connections to the Denver gang who runs the drug dealing show. When Jace quit dealing, Wolfe wanted to take over his "position" and when he didn't get to, he went for Jace's weakness – me. Jace continues, "Now that I'm on the UC team, I hear shit about other UC teams that most people never hear about. My teammates think the baseball team's taking steroids."

I gasp. Dramatically. I just can't help it.

Jace smiles at my reaction. "It's actually sorta commonplace with baseball teams, even in college. Based on how cagey a few guys have acted around me when that shit comes up, some of my teammates must know that Wes is dealing. Dennison's reaction at my comment about Wes tells me what I need to know."

"And mentioning the MLB? What was that about?"

"Just reminding him what's at stake. More than his status on campus, that's for sure."

A threat. And if Jace is right about the steroids, it's not a threat Clayton will be taking lightly. Hopefully that means Clayton won't bother me again. A lot was accomplished by that little exchange. I kiss Jace on the cheek before realizing he doesn't look pleased with his discovery. "Isn't it at least some relief that Wes isn't into the other stuff you guys were doing?"

"He's my brother, Pep. He's hurting. I know it and this shit he's doing is dumb and destructive. I've gotta help him. What do I do?"

I snuggle into his chest. "I don't know. Can you make him work for your dad somehow?"

"I'll try," he replies.

And then the drummer hits the beat and we're swept away into the music. We can't dance from our seated position, but we snuggle together, swaying to the rhythm. Jace gets restless after a couple songs and swings me onto his shoulders so he can be on his feet while keeping pressure off my legs.

It's hard not to enjoy good music from Jace's shoulders like this, despite the pain in my legs. Bodies swing and bounce to the rhythm and my view lets me take it all in. My head and arms have a life of their own as I try to let go of the fear and pain from the day. The music takes over, and Jace's strong hands grasping my ankles ground me in a way I didn't know I needed. Without his steady shoulders beneath me, I'm not sure how I'd be facing the truth: my running goals have been crushed. And perhaps not just for this season. I may have even jeopardized my chances at a scholarship to UC, which seemed like a sure thing only this morning.

But just when I start to feel suffocated by self-pity, the band starts in on an upbeat tune. I'm so tempted to jump down and get my groove on – I love dancing – but instead I lean forward to kiss Jace's head. When the band finishes its first set, Jace lifts me off his shoulders and places me back up on the ledge. It's past bedtime, and the day has taken its toll. Jace senses my exhaustion. We silently agree it's time to head out. He's got early morning practice anyway.

"Come on, I'll bring you home." He gestures for me to hop on his back, and I decide that having an injury has some perks after all.

"What about Wes?" I ask as Jace makes his way through the crowd.

"We'll find him."

I'm not so sure. Wes tends to take off whenever there are crowds around. Often with a girl, but apparently he also has other things that preoccupy him these days.

I see him first, standing by the stage with his head lowered, talking to Clayton Dennison. When Jace's arms stiffen around me, I know he's spotted Wes too. He starts to head in the opposite direction.

"We should go over there, Jace. Don't you want him to know you know what's up? Don't you want Clayton to know, too?"

He takes me down off his back so he can speak to me. It's too hard to hear him otherwise. I suppress a cringe when my feet hit the floor. It's not just my shins. Everything hurts.

"You okay?" Jace puts an arm around my waist to steady me and when I nod, he proceeds to half carry me toward the exit. I don't fight his coddling. He's taken some of the weight off my shins, and I'm grateful.

"I don't feel like dealing with it tonight, Pep. I came here to relax and enjoy time with you. For you to take your mind off shit."

"Well, Wes and Clayton's 'shit' is a distraction, at least."

Jace smiles grimly. "There's that, I guess. But the band's not bad, huh?"

We talk about the music until we're outside, when he crouches down and I happily climb onto his back. I'm dreading going back to my apartment. Just thinking of being alone in my small bedroom makes me feel suffocated. Dave will be there, but so will the pain in my legs and the dread of what it means. I probably won't be able to fall asleep and I'll end up on the Internet, typing into Google the words I've been avoiding searching for weeks. And I'm so scared of what I'll find. What if I've done permanent damage? I haven't even been thinking beyond this season and what it might mean for my scholarship to UC. But what if I can't run competitively ever again?

Jace glances at me, and I notice I'm practically shaking and gasping for air. He's transferred me from his back to the passenger seat, and I don't even remember it happening. He takes my hand, driving one-handed, and I realize he must've forgiven me for the Ryan/Gage episode last night. Or maybe there was nothing to forgive in the first place. Either way, we're past it.

When he pulls into his parking spot by the dorm, I start to breathe normally. The relief that I'm staying with him tonight, that I won't be alone, soothes me. Jace treats me like a child as he carries me inside, nodding to his roommates and the soccer girls. I glance over his shoulder and see the same scene from the other night, but without Savannah. Jace closes and locks his door before quietly undressing me, handing me one of his softest tee shirts, and tucking me into bed. He follows close behind, pulling me onto his chest. We don't talk, but his presence alone comforts me and protects me from the grief that's settling into my bones.

Losing my goals, my dreams, my *identity*... it's too much to bear alone. Running is who I am. It's what I do to think. To feel. But it's also just habit. Like brushing my teeth. Something will always feel off, all day and every day, if I don't go for a run. Jace's heavy arms are tightly wound around me and he's telling me without words that everything will be all right. I drift to sleep, trying to believe him.

Chapter 14

Jace can't miss class so it's just me and Gran at the doctor together. They do an x-ray and a bone density scan and then leave me waiting in the tiny room with Gran. I've turned my phone off, not wanting to deal with my teammates, or anyone else, asking for updates. Gran is engrossed in a celebrity gossip magazine and I'm jealous she finds it so fascinating. None of the magazines are sufficiently distracting for me right now. I haven't eaten a thing all morning, yet I still feel like I might throw up at any moment. Apparently shin pain and pregnancy have the same symptoms. Good thing I don't have to worry about the latter as a possibility.

Finally, Dr. Kennedy returns to our room. She introduced herself before the tests and went over some questions with me. I liked her immediately, and decided I would trust her diagnosis. After all, it still hurts to walk this morning. Again. The jig's up.

"I know you are a very competitive runner, Pepper, and that this must be hard for you," she begins. "So I'll just get right to it. You have bone marrow edema in your left tibia, and severe shin splints in your right tibia."

"What does that mean?"

"It means you don't quite have stress fractures yet, but your left leg nearly has one, and your right leg is headed in that direction as well."

I let out a breath I didn't know I was holding. Deep down, I knew I would hear something like this. But it doesn't make hearing it okay.

"How long until I can start training again?"

"The healing process for this injury usually requires six to eight weeks of rest."

Mercifully, Gran remains silent. She knows I'm already kicking myself. Six weeks puts me in mid-November. I might be able to make it to the state meet! But even if I can run by then, I'll be totally out of shape and there's no way I'll qualify for Regionals a week later. Regionals is the qualifying meet for Nationals, which is the second week in December. I can't decide whether to feel devastated or hopeful. I have avoided learning anything about my condition before today, and I wasn't sure if I'd be out for days or months. I suppose I thought months were more likely.

Renewed hope – realistic or not – takes a hold of me, and I revel in it.

"I spoke with your coach briefly before your appointment today, and I've agreed to meet with you and him to discuss the course of treatment and how it will impact your training. With your consent of course," she says, nodding at me and Gran.

"How it will impact my training? So, I'll still be training in some capacity?"

"Oh, yes. No running, of course. And I'd like you to take a few days completely off from any form of exercise to start. Also, you'll be using crutches for ten days to keep weight off your left shin."

"Crutches? Are you sure? I just ran my fastest 5K time ever… I'm not sure that's really necessary." Crutches are for people with broken legs and ankles. Not me. I'll still be training. She just said so. I'll still be an active athlete.

"Just for ten days. It will accelerate the healing process, and have you back out running faster."

She knows how to sell me on the crutches. I'll do anything to be back out running faster.

After picking up my crutches, promising to forgo exercise until Saturday (gulp!), and arranging a time to meet with Dr. Kennedy and Coach Tom tomorrow, Gran takes me to Clyde's Creamery. It's only just opened for the day, but unlike when the boys dragged me here last night, I have an appetite now. We order chocolate milkshakes and sit outside on the picnic table together.

"How does it feel?" Gran asks.

"The crutches?" I ask. "They're all right, I guess."

"I didn't mean the crutches," Gran says.

The kernel of hope that maybe I will recover from this in time to go to Nationals is barely alive, but it's there. "Do I give up for the season, Gran? I don't want to let go of the hope that maybe I can come back from this before it's over."

Dr. Kennedy did say that I may need longer than eight weeks, and I shouldn't expect to just up and start training at the level I'm used to when I finally do get out running again. But I mostly held onto her words that six weeks might be sufficient. And that would give me four weeks of running before Nationals. As I think more seriously about this timeline, and the measly four weeks I'll have to prepare even if I do qualify, the kernel of hope dwindles to the size of the tip of a needle. It hardly exists at all.

I share my fears with Gran. "I'm scared that it will hurt that much more if I do all the cross training and everything I'm supposed to do, only to be told I still can't run until the season's over. Or, what if I do get to run at State, but I do horribly because I haven't been running, and I don't qualify for Regionals?"

"You want to know what I think?" Gran asks. "I'm no athlete, but you just said you don't want to give up hope before the season's over, so don't. I saw how you were during track season last spring. You weren't your best self, Pep," she says with a knowing look. And then she shrugs. "You're special. And you're special because you are your best when you focus on a goal. When you do everything you can to get that goal. You maybe went about it a little too aggressively this time, but this new approach might just be your ticket. So no way, girl, am I telling you to give up when the goin' gets tough. It ain't over. You heard the lady. She's gonna talk to your coach, get a plan and all that."

I'm grinning so widely at Gran I feel like my face will break.

"Just be smarter this time. Do what that doctor and the coach tell you to do. Don't run before they say you should. And maybe you'll get where you want after all." She winks. "You're a fighter, Pep."

Her words get me through the rest of the day. As expected (and the reason I didn't want them), the crutches draw a lot of attention. If people didn't know already, everyone is now aware that I'm injured, and that it's bad. The hardest part of the day, though, is when I make my way over to the team's meeting spot by the baseball field dugouts. Even though it takes a while on crutches, I'm the first one there. Everyone else had to go to the locker room first to change. Coach Tom and the assistant coach, Janet, watch me approach.

135

"Don't look at me like that," I tell them, holding my chin high.

They attempt to wash their face of emotion, but I can tell the sight of me on crutches breaks their hearts a little.

"Coach, this is my fault. I ran more than you wanted me to. A lot more," I add, when he doesn't appear angry. He still shows no reaction; I have a feeling he already suspected as much. "But now I'm going to do everything I can to recover as quickly as possible, and I hope you'll be with me on it." I need him now, more than ever. I need him to believe in me.

"After you gave permission, I spent some time on the phone with Dr. Kennedy," he tells me. "Getting back out there this season is a long shot, Pepper, but I'm willing to work with you and the doctor to get you there, if you are willing to do what it takes." He hasn't said he believes I can do it, but he's never been one to encourage unrealistic hopes. It *is* a long shot. There's no doubt about it.

"I'll do everything it takes."

"No exercise until Saturday?"

I nod my agreement.

"We'll talk tomorrow with Dr. Kennedy about what happens after that. I don't expect you to show up to practice this week just to watch. Go home and get some rest."

It's pointless to be here today because it's a recovery day from yesterday's workout. Everyone will be dividing into small groups to go on easy runs, and I'll be left sitting here on my own. But I wait for my teammates anyway. I owe them an explanation. Miracles might happen, but I promise them nothing about me returning this season. It's weird making an announcement that's only about me, but my team deserves to know the truth about my injury. They shouldn't have to find out from school rumors.

The guys' team is there too, and I'm all too aware that Ryan's brother, Kevin, will likely report this news to his dad. UC doesn't make its first round of scholarship offers until the end of November, and I still have time to prove that this injury hasn't obliterated my chances of a successful collegiate running career.

I'm not expecting to hear anything from the head coach of the UC running team, but when I don't get any worried calls from Ryan that day, or the next day, or any day for the next week, I start to worry that I majorly hurt his feelings. It'd be nice to talk to him about what's going on. Yeah, it's annoying he'd be able to say he told me so and all that, but I'm sure he'd be helpful with weighing in on my new cross training routine.

I make a commitment to show up at the beginning of practice every day, even if it's painful. I'm still the captain, and I still need to be a leader on the team. Once I'm allowed to start pool running again I'll just stay for announcements and stretches.

Saturday is another meet, and watching from the sidelines on crutches is not something I'm looking forward to. As we often do before a meet, we head to Lou's after practice on Friday for a pasta dinner. Loading up on carbohydrates is really only necessary in preparation for an endurance event that lasts more than an hour or two, and our races are about twenty minutes. But carbo-loading before a race is tradition, whether we need the extra boost on race day or not. Lou's is a pizza joint owned by Kayla Chambers's family, but it also has inexpensive pasta dishes. I haven't been to Lou's since our run-in with Kayla at the party, but it's not like she's ever there anyway.

We squeeze seven of us into a booth that is probably more suitable for four people. It's just me, Zoe, Jenny, Rollie, Omar, and two juniors on the boys' team. It's nice to hang with my teammates, who are more interested in talking about running than Brockton gossip. Despite the regret that I won't be racing with them tomorrow, I'm enjoying myself.

Jenny will be the number one runner on the team in my absence. She's a firecracker and her positive energy is contagious. She's picked Madonna on the jukebox and is belting out the lyrics with gusto from her seat between me and Zoe. The whole table is entertained, and probably the surrounding tables as well. I notice Rollie watching her with a smile I've never seen on him before. Is Roland Fowler smitten with Jenny Mendoza? If so, I fully support that.

The door jingles as another group enters Lou's. The place is packed with students, families, and people just getting off work. I notice Omar and Rollie glance at the doorway, then at each other, and then at me. I frown at their reactions before turning around to see Wesley Jamison standing there with two guys who appear to be in their late twenties. All three of them are wearing jeans, work boots, and dirty tee shirts. It's not Wes's typical attire.

When he sees me, he grins, and makes his way to our table. "Hey Pep!" he greets me, and then my friends, though he doesn't know all of their names. They all know who he is, of course.

He introduces us to the two guys hovering beside him, who show little interest in socializing with high schoolers. Apparently they are his new co-workers at Brockton Construction Company. Well done, Jace.

"So, what are you guys up to tonight?" Wes asks the table.

"Just watching a movie at Rollie's house," I respond for the group. "Meet tomorrow." I don't have to tell him I won't be racing. The crutches leaning against the side of our booth tell him all he needs to know.

The next thing I know, Wes has invited us all over to his house, where he has a home theater, and plans have been made to show up there in an hour. I'm still contemplating the strangeness of the situation when we settle into the comfortable chairs with popcorn and water bottles (yup, hydrating is the top priority).

Wes and I have the back row chairs. "So you invited all my friends over to your house. What's up with that?" I can't help it. I'm suspicious.

Wes grins sheepishly at me through the darkness. "I haven't hung out with you in a while and I heard about what Gage shithead said. I'm not going to fuel that fire by hanging out with you alone again." Jace is in Utah for a football game tonight, so the three of us couldn't hang out. But inviting all my friends over is a bit much. As long as we didn't show up where all the Sig Beta guys hang out, I seriously doubt spending time with Wes would start more rumors. Though I suppose that's not something I want to deal with either.

"Plus, I kind of like your friend Zoe," Wes murmurs.

I glare at him. That's the real reason.

"What?" He holds up his hands innocently in response to my death glare. "You asked me to chaperone her at some party and I did that without making a move. I'm being cool running it by you before just going for it, aren't I?"

"So if I told you to lay off you would?" I ask.

"Yeah, obviously. She's just a cute girl who seems cool, Pep. But she's your best girlfriend. I'm not gonna mess with all that."

"That's the problem though, Wes. She's just a cute girl. You'll just want to hook up once, and then it will be all weird and awkward."

"It might be more than once," Wes says in all seriousness. "And besides, I hang out with girls I've slept with all the time. I'm excellent at not being weird and awkward about it."

Zoe can hold her own, and she knows as well as anyone that Wes doesn't do girlfriends. I should probably just stay out of it. "Do what you want," I tell him, "just don't put me in an awkward position."

By the end of the night, Rollie and Jenny have disappeared together (after Wes caught them cuddling and whispered what I presume was directions to a nearby room) and Wes and Zoe weren't far behind them. It's just Omar and the two juniors I'm not especially close with.

Wes's house is gigantic and it's almost always empty. Except for him. His parents are rarely home. They have a second home in LA, which has become more like their first home as far as I can tell. Wes is lonely, there's no doubt about it.

By the time the movie ends, the couples haven't returned. The four of us hang out chatting about the movie, the race tomorrow, and finally, that we should probably head home and get some sleep. I don't need it for the race, but I'm trying to get nine hours every night. Dr. Kennedy said the more rest, including sleep, the better.

This is my first night of the week not sleeping over in Jace's dorm room. I haven't wanted to be alone with my thoughts, and honestly, I sleep better with him beside me, which is saying something given the size of his dorm room bed. It's starting to dawn on me though just how weird it is that we sleep together but aren't sleeping together like *that*.

When we first got together, Jace was intent on taking things slow, and eventually I learned that was okay. But now it's been nearly a year and it's like neither of us wants to bring it up again. We've done everything *but* sex, and it's sort of become this line that we mutually decided we wouldn't cross for some reason. But we never really decided. It just became habit to not go there. With Jace's history before me, I don't know how he's done it. Me, I've almost gotten used to it. Like this is just the way it is. But everyone assumes we're having sex – even Zoe stopped prodding me about it. She thinks it happened and I just decided to keep it private.

My bed feels lonely without a warm body beside me. Correct that. A warm *human* body beside me. Dave is snoring happily, pressed up against the back of my legs, occasionally growling in his sleep. I miss Jace, and that simple thought makes me wonder why we've held back this part of ourselves. We've given everything else. What are we afraid of?

Chapter 15

I knew that cheering for my teammates while I was sidelined would be tough, but I didn't think it'd be this tough. As I watch on my crutches, three girls in the lead pass by, battling to be the first to the finish. Jenny isn't far behind with a pack, which quickly spreads out as the finish line comes into view and some kick it up a notch while leaving others in the dust. Zoe is holding her own, finishing within the top twenty of at least a hundred runners. She attempted to rehash the night with Wes on our drive here this morning, but I shut her up. If it was another guy it wouldn't be weird, but I know Wes too well for that.

The pain in my shins has dissipated over the past few days, but the pain in my chest and stomach is fully revived in this moment. It's twisting and sharp, and makes it hard to breathe, but not in the way I want. I want to feel a burn in my chest from sprinting to the finish.

I'd rather go home and sulk by myself but I swing myself with my crutches to the finish line to talk to my teammates. And now I have to hang here alone while the girls warm down and the boys race. How many more of these races will I have to endure on the sidelines? It's excruciating. I'd rather endure the shin pain if I could get away with it and keep running. But I know that's impossible.

"Pepper, how are you?" The concerned voice of Mark Harding startles me. He's standing in front of me, but I was clearly in my own world and didn't notice his approach.

"Mr. Harding, hi. I'm okay," I say, wondering what he thinks about seeing me on crutches. Does he know what happened? It seems like everyone else does.

"We are really looking forward to your official visit next weekend," he tells me with a smile.

How in the world did I manage to forget about that?

"Me too!" I respond eagerly.

"Well, I better cheer on Kevin. You take care of yourself, all right?"

"Of course."

When he walks away, I notice Ryan standing by the sidelines with his mom. He didn't even come over to say hi. But it doesn't bother me. Not when the head coach just told me he's looking forward to my recruiting trip. I got the feeling he was trying to tell me more with that statement. That maybe it's okay I'm injured. UC is still interested. And with that, my mood isn't so sour.

My spirit continues to lift when I finally get in my swimsuit and pool run for the thirty minutes pre-approved by Coach Tom and Doctor Kennedy. My shins are still a little tender when I put any weight on them, but pool running helps loosen them up.

Zoe texted me about a party tonight while I was in the pool, but as usual, I'm not in the mood. Tonight I want to keep resting, get to bed early, and maybe get my homework done. Jace returns from Utah tomorrow, and I want to have my day free for him. I'm not sure how to tell him I'm ready – *more* than ready – to finally be together in the one way we haven't yet.

As I leave the locker room and glance up from texting Zoe back, I see a group of athletic guys standing by the water fountains. And one blonde head catches my attention. Wes. I quickly scan the rest of the group, and I recognize one of the others as the guy at the concert with Clayton the other night.

Instinct tells me to walk on by (or swing by, since I'm still on crutches), but it's too late. I've been spotted. Someone says something to Wes, who turns around to find me. Instead of the easy smile he usually greets me with, his expression is tight. He is not happy to see me.

"Hey, Pepper," he says. "Pool workout?"

"Yeah," I say quietly. "I'm cross training for now."

"You got a ride home?" he asks.

"Gran should be here," I tell him, though she'll probably be another few minutes. She ran to the grocery store while I was swimming.

"Okay, cool, see you later then." And with that, he turns around.

Typically Wes would offer to walk me out, say hi to Gran, and generally just be friendlier. But if Jace's suspicions are right about Wes's activities, it's probably for the best he's keeping me at a distance. I want nothing to do with it.

Gran's car isn't in the parking lot, so I settle myself onto a bench and start checking email on my phone. When I sense a looming presence in front of me a moment later, I glance up. Gage Fitzgerald.

He's not dressed to work out and isn't carrying a bag or anything, and I vaguely wonder why he's at the gym. But my main thought is why he's stopped in front of me, eyeing me with interest.

"What do you want?" I ask.

"No company this time?"

"No," I respond tightly.

"Take it easy, Pepper Jones, I'm only joking." He flashes a grin. "And tell your boyfriend to chill out too. You know I was only messing around the other night, and I was drunk."

I stay quiet. Is he trying to apologize? If so, it's a lame apology. I'm not even sure which night he's talking about. He acted like an asshole on two occasions.

"Wilder shouldn't take himself so seriously. He's only a freshman. Get him to come out sometimes. He's always welcome. You too," he adds with a wink.

When I still don't respond, and just raise my eyebrows at him, Gage shrugs and walks to the entrance of the gym. The guy really doesn't get it. I don't control Jace, and even if I did have some influence over how he spent his time, there's no reason I'd encourage him to go to a Sig Beta party, especially not after Gage insulted me in front of a crowd. Twice. The dude must be delusional.

Ten minutes later, and still no Gran. She must have started reading cards in the stationery aisle at the store. She does that sometimes and ends up losing track of time. I've caught her there giggling to herself at the card jokes.

People come and go without noticing me; I'm about to call Zoe to see if she can come get me, when Wes walks by with Gage at his side. Wes nods and flashes that tense smile he gave me earlier, but he doesn't stop to chat. I watch him get into the passenger side of Gage's SUV, and I know I'm witnessing something I'm not supposed to. Before I can contemplate what it all means, Gran has pulled up in front of me and is calling out the window, apologizing for being late. Something about a man named Harold who needed a ride back to the nursing home.

"He's quite the looker for a guy in his eighties," she's telling me as she pulls out of the parking lot. I glance at the back of the SUV as we pass. Something is going down. It doesn't involve me, but in some ways, it feels like it does. Wes might not be my brother, best friend, or boyfriend. He doesn't have a label for who he is to me, but he matters. Gran, Zoe, Wes, Jace – they are my family. But I'm not sure how I can help him.

When Jace was going down a bad path last year, Wes told me that just being *there* for Jace made a difference. I was his rock. Still am, I guess. But that's not how I am for Wes, and I don't know if Wes has anyone in his life whose presence alone can bring him back. Because he's drifting away. Somehow, underneath his friendliness at the diner, his invitation to my friends last night, his typical ladies-man habits, I get a strange feeling we're losing him. Even though he stayed in Brockton, he feels farther away than ever.

Gran and I have a quiet dinner at home and she invites me to join her and Lulu to see a movie, but I opt for a phone call with Jace instead. I miss him. They won the game against Utah, and their record is off to a better start than it has been in years. The news stations are saying that's thanks to Jace, and I'm tremendously proud of him. His own success helps ease the pain of my failures.

A moment after hanging up with Jace, there's a knock at our front door. It's usually unlocked when one of us is home but sometimes on weekends we lock it at night. We share the building with college kids and their visitors frequently go to the wrong apartment on the weekends. I'm anticipating an encounter with a confused college student when I open the door, but instead it's Wes.

He's still wearing the workout clothes he was in earlier. I gesture for him to come inside.

"No crutches?" he asks.

"Not around the apartment. My legs are feeling better anyway." Our apartment is tiny, so as soon as walking became mostly pain-free, I stopped trying to clamber around the place with crutches. It's my only cheating so far, but I think Coach would understand.

I plop down in the living room armchair, and he follows suit on the couch. I know he came here to say something, so I wait for him to break the silence. Wes puts his hands on his knees.

"I'm sorry about earlier," he says with genuine regret in his voice.

"What exactly are you apologizing for?" I knew he was being stand-offish to protect me, so I don't need an apology.

"For making you worry about me. For being stupid enough to start dealing again. But today I fixed it. I hope."

"Yeah?" Now I'm curious.

"Gage Fitzgerald is the new 'roid dealer on campus," Wes announces.

"You're out?" I'm relieved. Wes's relapse to drug dealing (if it can even be called that) was short-lived before he saw the error of his ways.

"Not only that, but one of the conditions of Gage getting my supplier's contact was that he has yours and Jace's backs."

My eyes narrow. "What exactly does that mean?"

"He'll stop bugging Jace to be a Sig Beta social symbol or whatever the hell he thinks Jace can do for him, and he'll stop being an asshole when he doesn't get what he wants." So he won't use me to get to Jace. That's one less person, at least.

"You must have told him this after you left the gym," I say dryly.

Wes's jaw clenches the same way Jace's does when he's angry. "Why? What did he do?"

"Nothing," I say on a sigh. "Some attempt at an apology for being a jerk and then telling me I should get Jace to stop taking himself so seriously and come out and have fun."

Wes relaxes a little and then shakes his head. "He can be a real idiot when he's fucked up, which I've noticed is frequently. But yeah, I talked to him about the terms after we left the gym. Him saying stupid shit to you isn't the most important term, though."

"What's that?"

"He'll keep Clayton Dennison in check."

"Gage Fitzgerald will keep Clayton Dennison in check? Gage is mister fraternity hot shot on campus and Clayton is mister athlete hot shot. How is one supposed to keep the other in check?"

"Clayton's not the hot shot he used to be. Some guy named Jace Wilder is now the hottest athlete on campus."

I roll my eyes. "That's not what I'm getting at."

"Gage will be dealing to Clayton and his team. He can use that in a lot of ways. For starters, he can stop dealing to them. Or he can out the team. Gage has the connections to really fuck up Clayton's MLB chances."

"What's Clayton's problem anyway? Jace doesn't even go out. He's all football. And me," I add with a sweet smile.

"And you," Wes agrees with a laugh before getting serious again. "Jace's lack of partying is only working to give him a sense of allure and mystery."

That makes me laugh. Hard. Because I have to say, it really doesn't surprise me. My boyfriend does nothing but go to class, train, sleep, and hang out with me and his parents. Yet this only makes the guys admire him more and the girls want him more.

Wes laughs with me. "He's always had that though, hasn't he?"

My laughter fades. It's true. Before he started seeing me romantically, Jace's mysteriousness was dark. It wasn't so much a mystery to me – I knew that underneath his coolness, his leadership, there was sadness and pain from his mom's abandonment. That's not something that goes away. I don't know if it was his mom returning or me getting closer to him, but the sadness and pain seems to have disappeared. Sometimes I fear they are just hiding, but my hope is those feelings will continue healing with time.

"Anyway," Wes continues, "even if the campus wasn't fascinated by Jace Wilder, the media attention has crowned him UC's savior – in football at least, after the last couple games. Dennison's a really competitive dude. He doesn't like another guy taking the spotlight. Not when he's had it for a couple years now."

I nod, beginning to understand. "It's like a repeat of his junior year at Brockton," I reflect. "He was expecting to be the king of the school, but Jace came along as a freshman and tainted it for him."

"Dennison's been carrying a giant two by four on his shoulder about Jace Wilder ever since," Wes agrees.

We head into the kitchen to make hot chocolate, Wes checking a text while I get out the mugs. My phone buzzes a minute later.

Zoe: I invited Wes to the party. I shouldn't really expect him to show tho, right?

Sighing, I glance at Wes. I don't want to play any role with Zoe and Wes, two of my closest friends. No one wants to be put in that position. But Wes thrives in social environments, and I sort of feel like celebrating his accomplishment today. A high school party probably isn't his first choice, but Wes is so easy going that as long as there are people, drinks, and a girl he's interested in around, he'll be down. This is being a good friend, right? Hanging alone with me on a Saturday night would just make him feel lonelier than he already is.

"Should we go check out this party?" I ask.

"Up to you, Pep. You look like you were planning on a night in," he says and gestures to my yoga pants and slippers.

"I was about to go to sleep," I admit. It's almost ten, which is my bedtime on school nights. Turns out I'm not so bad at this resting business.

Except, we do end up heading over to the party. We put the hot chocolate in to-go mugs, and Wes pours some liquor from Gran's cabinet in his. Me, I just top it with whipped cream. The address is in Wes's gated community, ironically, and it's actually hosted by a girl who goes to Wes's old high school, Lincoln Academy.

Neither of us has changed our clothes, but I don't think that's the only reason everyone turns to stare at us when we walk into the kitchen. It's an exclusive party, something I should have realized right away by the few cars parked outside. And aside from perhaps Zoe, it's a wealthy crowd. The clothes alone tell me that.

Omar and Rollie must not have made the cut, because the only other Brockton Public people are Dana Foster, Tina Anderson and Diego Thompson. Zoe looks relieved to see me, and I can tell it's not only because Wes is with me. She might be a social butterfly, but she knows this isn't her crowd, and she'd much prefer having Brockton Public kids surrounding her.

Wes either senses Zoe's anxiety or remembers the rumors spreading about him and me because he heads right to her and places his arms on her waist in greeting. Some of the tension in the room eases when he does this and I realize that Wes and I showing up in workout/sleep clothes together late on a Saturday night when everyone knows the football team is away was probably a very bad idea. Hopefully Wes recognizes this faux-pas as well and makes out very publicly with Zoe. She didn't exactly warn me this "party" was a get together with only a dozen people.

A girl with a short stylish haircut introduces herself and offers me a drink. I hold up my mug and tell her I'm fine. She keeps eyeing Wes, and it hits me why she looks familiar. I saw Wes with her at a party last year. Well, I'm sure he's been in a room with more than one girl he's hooked up with before. And since she's clearly the host and Wes's neighbor, Wes knew exactly what he was getting himself into before we came inside. It's not my problem, I remind myself.

With Zoe and Wes together and conversation resuming in the huge kitchen, I join Dana and Diego, who are talking with a couple of Lincoln Academy guys. I still don't consider Brockton Public's popular people my friends, but we've associated enough this semester for me to be comfortable mingling with them for a couple of hours.

"What do you think, Pepper Jones?" One of the guys, whom I don't think I've ever met, acknowledges that I've joined the conversation.

"Think about what?"

"A guy on our team," he says, as though I should know what team he's on, "has been with this girl for like, six months, and they haven't slept together yet. That's weird, right?"

I almost drop my mug of hot chocolate. The question hits way too close to home. It was a really bad idea to come here tonight.

When I don't answer right away, his friend jumps in, "I mean, this is high school, right, and the dude's a senior. He either needs to lose the v-card with this girl ASAP or break up with her and find someone else because he can't be a virgin in college."

The logical side of me is saying these guys are idiots. But the emotional side of me is panicking. How in the world did Jace wait this long? Why? Is something wrong between us? Ten months. That's how long we've been together.

Diego, Dana, and the two idiots look at me, expecting some sort of response. I shrug, afraid too strong of a reaction will give me away. "I have no idea who you're talking about so can't say I have much of an opinion about his virginity."

The guys laugh, even though it wasn't funny, and begin talking about something else that is also probably none of their business.

I can just imagine the shock if people discovered I was still a virgin after ten months with Jace Wilder. But I'm hoping that will change soon, as long as I can convince Jace the decision is on my terms, and not because of his background or because of what people would say. Though I don't like thinking that many girls have had what I have not, that's not why I want him. There's no one else I want to be with like that. Just Jace.

Chapter 16

Showing up at the gym on crutches is weird, no doubt about it. But the thing is, there are a lot of exercises you can do without putting pressure on your shins. Walking just isn't one of them. Sunday morning I go through the new weight lifting and exercise program that the trainer showed me. It's not very rigorous, but it will help maintain some of my running strength. Though I'm excited to work out, I find myself rushing through it in order to see Jace. The team flew back from Utah this morning and he should be back in his dorm by the time I'm done.

Jace must have missed me too, because his familiar Jeep is waiting in the gym parking lot when I head outside. It's only been three days since I last saw him, but it feels like weeks. He scoops me up and puts me in the passenger seat before pulling out of the parking lot with unexpected urgency.

"In a hurry?" My first guess is that he's hungry. That usually gets him moving.

He flashes a smile that I like to think is reserved for me. It's full of promises and mischief. "Yes," he simply replies. "We're going to Shadow Lane. Dad's out of town with Sheila this weekend."

My heart rate immediately picks up. Has he been having the same thoughts as I have? His bed at his dad's is bigger, and with Jim gone, it will be much more private than his dorm.

"I have some stuff I need to grab and I figured you could take a shower there if you want," he explains. Well, maybe he doesn't have ulterior motives, but I do.

When he turns onto Shadow Lane and pulls into his driveway, the rightness of this time and place sinks in. We made it through the transition from friends to more. We stayed strong through high school and we've grown stronger since college started. I feel like Jace and I can face anything together. Coming back here now, after so much has happened between us, I'm confident we waited until the right moment. We know who we are. Together and apart.

Jace suspects there's something on my mind when we descend the stairs and head into his bedroom together. It's dark down here, but the natural light streaming in from the window is enough. I stop Jace from turning on the overhead light.

"No, I want to keep it this way," I say meaningfully.

I tug him close and trace along his jawline, watching his green eyes blaze as they take me in, studying my body language. *I want you.* That's what I'm thinking and what my body is feeling. And there's little doubt that Jace has understood the message when he closes his eyes briefly, letting me take control. It's usually him leading the way. And that's how I like it. But right now, I need to tell him with my touch what I want. Slowly, I undress completely until I stand before him with nothing on. The heat between us, and the promise in his gaze, is all I can think about.

I let him drink me in before tugging his clothes off. He's already ready for me but I lead him to his attached bathroom, turning on the shower. We've been patient for ten months now, or is it our entire lives? We can take a quick rinse together first.

As we help wash each other, I'm glad I already told him that I've been on birth control since we started dating. Gran's idea. At least we don't have to bring that up now. Though I'm acting confident, my hands are shaking. My heart might be sure of this, but it's still scary. Jace takes my hands in his and turns off the shower.

"You know I would wait for as long as you wanted, Pepper," Jace says.

"And you know that I want this." I kiss him on the chest. "Now." Kiss on the chin. "Today." When my lips hit his, he lifts me up and carries me to his bed, somehow grabbing a towel and placing it underneath me on the way.

"I love you, Pepper Jones," Jace tells me as he leans forward, water dripping from his forehead onto mine. There's so much emotion in his voice, and he's not afraid to let me hear it.

Jace's mouth and hands run thoroughly over my body before he reaches for his bedside table to pull out a foil packet. Apparently he still keeps a stash of condoms here, but I don't let my mind linger on how that habit developed in the first place. Instead, I'm simply thankful he's prepared. Because I'm more than ready.

The initial contact is painful, which isn't a surprise, but Jace is smooth and slow, whispering tender words as he exercises as much control over his body as he can muster. His motions are restrained but filled with so much more than lust. The pain turns quickly to pleasure, and the joy at being this close with the boy I've loved for as long as I can remember sends me over the edge faster than I expect. Jace doesn't even try to prolong our first time and I don't know if he could. The expression on his face when he finishes with me is one I will always remember. It's happiness.

When I discover my cheeks are wet, and not from the shower, and Jace's eyes glisten in return, we both laugh at the absurdity of our response. "Why are we crying?" I say, my voice muffled in his shoulder as he rests beside me.

"I never understood happy tears until now," Jace tells me. He only shed one or two, but I'm a faucet.

This emotional response was not expected. I thought it would be much more overwhelming physically than emotionally. We've now shared everything two people can share, and it's incredible. I've never felt closer to anyone.

How in the world do people have casual sex? I wonder. But I quickly wipe that thought away, not wanting it to take my thoughts on a path that brings anyone else into this bed, this room, with us.

Jace and I stay at the house all day – mostly in his room – but we venture up to the kitchen a couple times. The day is filled with so much sweetness and tenderness, I don't know how either of us will return to the real world. So we don't. At least not until the next day.

The only phone call I make is to Gran to let her know where I am. Jace texts Frankie where he is and then we disappear into our own world.

***

"You really don't seem as depressed about your injury as I expected," Zoe tells me at lunch the following Friday.

158

I've essentially been beaming nonstop since Sunday. I shrug, but keep the smile plastered on my face. Zoe eyes me suspiciously, but I'm not going to divulge something so private, even to my best girlfriend. Maybe someday it will come up, but it's so fresh and magnificent. If I talk about it at the lunch table like it's any old gossip, it will undermine how important it is.

"Are you excited for the official visit tomorrow or what?" Zoe asks. It'll be me with a group of seven other running recruits for an overnight with the UC team. The others have likely never visited UC before, though.

"Yeah, I am. It'll be weird, though. I mean, I've probably already been to most of the places they'll take us on the tour. Sometimes I feel like I'm already a college student." I was going to the gym frequently before my injury, but now that my training is all in the pool and weight room, I'm at UC every morning and afternoon. I stop in for announcements with the team before biking over to campus. Zoe let me permanently "borrow" her bike as soon as I got off crutches and Coach said it's cool as long as I'm just riding to get around town and I don't ride up any major hills.

"Don't you spend, like, every night in Jace's dorm, too?" Tina Anderson has slid down the bench to join us.

"Most nights," I tell her. It's become more frequent. I come home to have dinner with Gran and to spend a little time doing homework, but I've been heading over to Jace's dorm almost every other night recently. It's the only time I get to see him during the week. He'll finally be on campus with no game this weekend, but I've got the official visit, so we don't get much time on the weekends either.

Tina expects me to elaborate about my nights with Jace, but given that I don't even disclose those details to Zoe, she's out of luck. Privacy is not a concept she understands. Sometimes I just want to turn it around on her and ask who she slept with recently and how it went, but I don't care enough. Besides, she might revel in disclosing the details of her sex life.

Ignoring Tina, Zoe asks what the agenda is for the recruit trip. "I'm not sure yet. Probably a group run that I can't participate in, a meal at the cafeteria, tour of campus, stuff like that. At least, that's all we did at Oregon."

"It's Saturday night though, right? Do they take you to parties or anything?" Tina pipes in.

"I doubt it. They'd probably get in trouble for exposing us to underage drinking or something. At Oregon we just hung out at a house a bunch of upperclassmen on the team lived in."

"That's dumb," Tina says. "I would want to know what the night life is like."

"The night life isn't really the reason athletes go to college, though, Tina," Zoe states the obvious.

"Well, I'm going to State. I haven't done my application yet, but my mom and aunt went there so I'll probably get in. I haven't gotten to see what the parties are like first hand, but it's got a reputation for being wild." Colorado State is a five-hour drive from Brockton, in the southwest corner of the state. About half of Brockton Public students go to UC in Brockton, maybe ten percent go to State, ten percent to Mountain West (where Charlie goes), and the rest either go out of state or don't go to college. Zoe's planning to apply to all three Colorado colleges.

"I'm just going to see who gives me the best financial aid," Zoe tells us. It's more complicated than that, but in the end a lot of the decision will come down to tuition costs. For both of us. If UC doesn't offer me a full scholarship and somewhere else does, that will be tough. College loans are not something I want to take on if I don't have to.

Tina decides our conversation is not juicy enough for her and slides back to the other end of the table. Once she's out of earshot, Zoe tells me, "If the team is cool with it, you should come out to a party at Kayla's sorority on Saturday night."

I never did tell Zoe about the incident with Kayla weeks ago. I'm not even sure I'd be welcome at a party at her place anyway. "She invited you to another party? Are you guys in touch or something?"

"No, I haven't talked to her since I saw her at that party at the beginning of the semester. But Wes invited me to go with him."

"Oh?" I can't hide my surprise. I've never known Wes to ask a girl to go to a party with him. Almost like a date.

"Yeah, at first I thought it was just a casual thing," she says, glancing around to make sure no one's listening. "But we've been texting all week, so, I don't know."

She's looking to me for some answers. Some guidance. But I am just as clueless as she is.

"I'm the last person who can help you with this, Zoe. I know I'm friends with Wes but I have no idea how he operates with the girls he hooks up with. And when it comes to casual hook-ups, I can't say I have any experience." She knows this already, but a reminder can't hurt. Just because I'm dating Jace Wilder doesn't mean his hook-up experience has been imparted to me somehow. People forget these things. They seem to assume I'm not only much cooler than I was before Jace and I got together, but that I'm much more knowledgeable about everything social. Not so much.

"Yeah, I don't have much experience here either. I'm trying not to overthink it, you know? But it's really hard not to imagine that maybe I'll be different for him. Maybe I'll be the girl who he wants to be serious with," she admits quietly.

Oh dear. This is not good. Not good at all.

Zoe reads my expression and laughs, but it's not as lighthearted a sound as usual. "Relax, Pep. I'm just being honest. Saying it aloud helps me realize how dumb it sounds. I mean really, it's not like it started out as anything special. I'll just try to keep it low key and fun, right?"

"Look Zoe, if you want more with him and you have feelings for him, you really need to be careful. As far as I know, this isn't anything serious for Wes, and I don't want you to get hurt."

She already looks hurt, just having what she already knows confirmed. I don't think she really likes him, not seriously. I mean, everyone likes Wes, and he's hot, but she's just wrapped up in the idea of him.

"Sometimes I just want a happily ever after like you and Jace," she tells me. "Is that so bad?"

Her words surprise me. I thought she broke up with Charlie because she wasn't up for so much commitment. "Didn't you have something good with Charlie? I didn't know you wanted a relationship."

"Yeah, I probably don't. You are just so in love and so happy with him it's hard not to want to be like that with someone too when I see you."

I can't deny it. I am definitely happy and in love. "You will be some day. But don't look for it where it doesn't exist. Don't force it." I'm not sure where that advice came from, but it's the best I can offer for the moment.

We both glance around when we sense a change in the atmosphere, the loud voices shifting to hushed murmurs. Zoe is looking at something behind me and I swivel around to see what it is. A guy is pushing a cart with a humongous vase of roses. Two dozen, I guess. And he's headed straight toward my table.

Chapter 17

When the delivery guy asks for a signature, I immediately ask if there's a card. There isn't. Knowing all eyes are on me, I pretend to be excited as I sniff and admire the roses. But as soon as the attention shifts away from me, I let my guard down.

"Zoe, even you have to know this is weird for Jace," I tell her in a hushed voice.

"Yeah, he's not really a showy guy. Did he do something wrong he's trying to make up for?" she asks and I shake my head. "Is this some sort of anniversary?" I shake my head again.

"I don't think Jace sent these," I say warily. Whoever did send them wanted it to be a spectacle.

"What do you mean? Of course it was Jace." Zoe looks at me like I'm crazy. "He's crazy about you and just wanted to send some love since you've been injured and stuff. Not that you've been all that depressed about it or anything," she adds.

It's possible Jace is just trying to be sweet, given what happened a few days ago. But my gut tells me otherwise. Jace isn't really a roses guy. He's sent me flowers in the past, and they were never roses. Too cliché. And showy. He knows I wouldn't want the attention from a delivery at the Brockton Public cafeteria. It just doesn't feel right.

Besides, what am I supposed to do with them for the rest of the day? It's not like they'll fit in my locker or my backpack.

We're not supposed to have cell phones in school so I can't call Jace right now, but I send him a quick text thanking him for the flowers. If it's not him who sent them, the text will make him flip his shit, but I have to know. The curiosity will kill me if I have to wait the rest of the day to find out.

My suspicion is confirmed when my phone vibrates during fifth period. I didn't send you flowers, Pepper. Call me ASAP.

I sneak into the bathroom and hit Jace on speed dial. He's fuming. "What kind of sick fuck sends my girlfriend two dozen roses?"

"We can call the flower shop to find out, right? I got the name of it."

I tell him the name of the shop, and he hangs up immediately to call. But they won't give him any information, explaining that the delivery was meant to be anonymous. I decide to try calling the shop myself after classes, but they are just as adamant about keeping the person's identity private. Whoever sent them gave very specific instructions.

The urge to run through the emotions pulsing through me is overwhelming. Although I'm still on crutches, it's so tempting to find my running shoes in my locker and *just go*. I'm pissed off, confused, and a little freaked out. The only way I know how to channel these feelings is to run hard and fast until I'm calmer. Pool running just doesn't have the same effect. It's too tame and I stare at the same four walls the entire time.

But my resolve to let my shins heal holds me back. There's still hope, even if it's faint, that I can get to Nationals. And if I can make it that far, anything can happen. The possibility of defending my title isn't completely lost. And for that, I have to let go of my urge to run.

I make it through the rest of classes, announcements and stretching with the team, pool running, and dinner with Gran. The only thing keeping me from busting out onto the trail is the anticipation of seeing Jace. After stuffing some homework into my backpack, I jump on my bike and take the familiar sidewalks to Jace's dorm.

It's already dark and even though there isn't much traffic on these streets this time of night, I stay on the sidewalk. I still haven't gotten around to getting a helmet. As the darkness settles and I turn onto a street without lamps, I realize I may need to get a bike light as well. The headlights from a car behind me help light the way, but when the car doesn't pass me after a moment, I start to feel a cold chill up my spine.

The street is empty except for me and this car, which is either thoughtfully lighting my path or driving super slowly because the driver is trying to find the right address. *Or following me.* The thought is ridiculous, but the car is still there as I turn onto a road through campus. Students come and go between buildings, but the car doesn't pass me. When I glance behind me, all I can see are the headlights.

Fear sets in and my legs pump harder. Adrenaline courses through me when I take the final turn to Jace's dorm and the car is still behind me. What if it's some crazy person preying on college girls? I've heard stories about people like that on college campuses. My mind swirls with possibilities until I see Jace waiting for me outside the building and relief floods through me. The car speeds past me as I slow to a stop. Squinting, I try to make out anything memorable about the vehicle. It's a white SUV with Colorado plates, which are already too far away to read. In the darkness, I can't make out much more than that.

Jace takes in my frenzied expression and pulls me to him. "Whoa, Pep, you okay?" Jace kisses my forehead and tilts up my chin to look at him.

The fear disappears and I suddenly feel silly. I'm just on edge from the flowers. The idea of a car following me is ridiculous. If it was, it was probably just because the driver thought I was someone they knew, and when they realized I wasn't they took off.

"Yeah, I'm fine, I just rode really fast to get here." I can tell Jace is already tense from the roses, and telling him I think I was being followed, when I'm probably just being paranoid, is a bad idea.

He locks up my bike and leads me upstairs. When we're alone in his room, I mold my body to his, seeking comfort.

"Tell me you trashed those flowers," Jace says.

"I gave them to the principal," I reply, already tugging at the hem of his shirt.

Jace laughs. "Good call."

He starts to say something about how he told Frankie, and they're going to figure out who sent the flowers, but I shush him. What I need right now is him. Jace understands my intent, and we spend the rest of the night together, with no words spoken about the flowers.

Spending the night in Jace Wilder's dorm room isn't exactly the same as sprinting up a hill as fast as I can, but it has a similar effect. When I close my eyes to fall asleep, Jace's arm draped lazily across me, my emotions are under control. The anger and confusion haven't disappeared entirely, but Jace's strength and love help wash them away from the surface so I can breathe freely again. His steady breathing beside me tells me that being with me helps to soothe his tension as well. Knowing this, I fall asleep with a smile on my face. We might have people against us, but they don't know what they're fighting against.

When I wake up the next morning, I decide the flower incident could have been anyone. Heck, it could have been a misguided freshman boy with an infatuation. "Let's just forget about it," I tell Jace. "If someone's trying to mess with us, the best thing we can do is shake it off."

Jace's body language tells me he doesn't want to let it go. He's tense as he loads my bike into his Jeep to take me home. "We'll see," is all he says.

The truth is, after what happened with Wolfe and Rex last year, I'm hesitant to let this go too. While it could be a harmless gesture, it could also be something more serious. Wolfe took his attack way too far. I've pushed it deep down and tried not to think about it, but his attempt to drag me to the pool house at a party one night still gives me nightmares. Though his intentions that night may have been only to scare me, something tells me I'd be naïve to believe that. Jace and Wes have told me that Wolfe won't bother us anymore, and I want to believe them. Unfortunately, the chill I felt last night as I rode my bike haunts me as Jace drives me back to Shadow Lane to pack a bag for the recruit trip.

When Jace drops me off in front of the admissions office, where I'll check in for the overnight visit, he tells me to call him if I have an opportunity to go out tonight. "They don't always know what to do with recruits on these official visits. They want to party, but unless the recruits give a clear green light that they won't tattle to the coaches or whatever, they have to stay in," Jace explains, having been a recruit himself, and now having participated on the other side of the process.

"I don't really know the girls on the cross team, but if they seem down, you guys should come over to an off-campus house party I've been talked into hitting up."

"Don't count on it," I warn him. "I'm not going to go rogue on this visit, Jace. It's important I'm perceived as a serious athlete. Someone they want on their team. Not some party girl."

"You won't, Pep," Jace says with a knowing smile. "Your running speaks for itself."

Except for the fact that I'm injured, and I can't count on my prior running results as a shoe-in anymore. I have to show I have what it takes to work through an injury and come out stronger. Patience and determination. Those are the qualities I need to convey right now. And it's not hard, because that's what I've been focusing on these last two weeks.

After checking in at the admissions office, I'm introduced to Sienna Darling, a petite junior who will be hosting me in the four-bedroom suite she shares with three other girls on the cross team. Three of the other recruits on the visit will be staying at the suite with her roommates.

I follow the team's results online, and I know that Sienna is one of their top runners. She's quiet and serious, but not at all shy. She carries my bag across campus with a confident stride. I'm feeling comfortable, like I could fit right in, until we enter her dorm room.

It's the building next to Jace's dorm, and the layout of the suite is nearly identical. There are six other girls in the room already when Sienna and I join them. Chatter stops and everyone turns to look at me. Silence. It's deafening.

Finally, Sienna introduces herself to the three other recruits before introducing me to them, as well as her other three roommates. But the staring doesn't stop, even as the girls shuffle off to the individual rooms to change for the group run.

My immediate thought is that the attention has something to do with Jace. Or Wesley. Or my injury. But some, if not all, of the girls have never heard of Jace Wilder or Wesley Jamison. I'm off my crutches and not limping, so unless news has spread nationwide (the other recruits are from Florida, Ohio, and New York), there's no reason for them to know about my injury. So it's just me.

It takes about ten minutes before I admit to myself that I'm famous to these girls. To a top high school recruit, and apparently even some top college runners, meeting me is like meeting a celebrity. It's difficult to swallow this knowledge. Their reaction to my presence is simultaneously empowering and disturbing. I'm really just a normal girl who runs fast.

While the other recruits go on a group run with the team, a freshman on the team named Lexi Bell takes me to a gym I've never been to before. Lexi is also injured so we're both relegated to cross training.

When I tell her I've been going to a different gym on campus, she tells me that's where the athletes who are off-season usually go to work out. "It's still mostly only people on sports teams who have access to that gym, but we're only supposed to use this one when we're in season. There's a little more variety in the equipment, and the trainers and coaches' offices are in this building," Lexi explains. "It's not like we all can't use both gyms, but it's an unofficial rule everyone tries to follow so that this gym doesn't get too crowded."

Lexi is one of those girls who can only be described as adorable. She has naturally curly hair that looks so fluffy and soft I want to touch it. With long eyelashes and a petite frame, I'm not surprised at the flirtatious smiles several guys in the gym send her way.

"Soccer teams must not have a game this weekend," she comments as she looks around the gym. For being the most exclusive weight room on campus, it's fairly busy.

"Oh yeah," Lexi recalls, "this is the big recruiting weekend because most teams don't have games for some reason." She nods as this information settles and then turns to me. "That's good. It means there should be some fun parties tonight that we can all go to."

"Really?" I'm surprised. "I would think it would be the opposite with recruits here."

"Nah, these parties will be just for teams with recruits so they'll be toned down. Only athletes will be there. I mean, that's what I hear at least. It wasn't like this when I came for my official visit last year. We just sat around talking all night. Not very exciting, but some of the high school seniors who come on these trips would freak if you took them to a frat party."

I giggle, thinking of some of the girls on my cross team. "I know what you mean."

I'm getting along well with Lexi, imagining that if I do come to UC (I hate that it's recently become an "if" not a "when"), we would be friends. We're both going through our own exercise routine on the various machines, chatting in between reps, and I'm looking forward to getting to know the other girls on the team. Hopefully everyone will be as easy to talk to as Sienna and Lexi.

We're winding down and getting ready to leave and I head over to the mat where Lexi is stretching to join her. Two girls are standing over her, and they are enormous compared to her. As I get closer, I realize it's Savannah the amazon woman and one of her roommates who hangs in Jace's common area. The one with pigtails. The other two who were there that night didn't seem as vicious, probably because they were preoccupied with the boys they liked.

But I don't back down now. Instead, I position myself beside Lexi and begin stretching my hamstrings. It's something I can do while still standing, which helps put me on their level. Well, they are both super tall so I'm more at shoulder height, but it's better than sitting down.

Lexi introduces pigtail girl, Veronica, and begins to introduce me to Savannah, who cuts her off. "We've met," she says coldly.

Lexi frowns. "Yeah, okay. Maybe we'll see you at Alberto's tonight then," Lexi says in a dismissive voice.

I'm impressed with her confidence in the midst of their intimidating stances.

"You know them?" I ask when they walk away.

"Not really," Lexi tells me as she watches them go. "I've run into them a few times working out or at the athletes' cafeteria, but we're not friends or anything."

"You're going to Alberto's tonight? Isn't that a bar?" It's the most popular college bar.

"Oh, yeah." She breaks her gaze away from Savannah and pigtail girl. "It's closed tonight to the public for a private party for all the recruits. I don't know why I'm only hearing about it now, but the cross girls don't spend a lot of time talking about party stuff, you know?"

"Which teams will be there?" I wonder.

She shrugs. "Beats me. Soccer at least, I know that."

But not football. Jace already told me about a different party for the football team. "Are they serving alcohol?" I mean it is a bar, after all, but it seems really stupid on the school's part to host an event that serves alcohol to high school seniors.

Lexi laughs. "Officially? Only to those of us with IDs," she says with a glint in her eye. By the way she said "us", I have a feeling Lexi is one of the more rebellious girls on the team.

Tonight might be more fun than I thought. As long as I keep my distance from the amazon.

Chapter 18

The Dean of Athletics makes an announcement during dinner at the athletes' cafeteria. He greets the recruits, talks about how honored UC is to have us, and highlights all the benefits of coming to his school. Before sending us off for the night, he makes clear that he expects the students to be good representatives of the athletic program tonight, and that there will be no underage drinking. It's hard to tell if anyone is taking him seriously, but I for one will not be jeopardizing my chances at a scholarship. Everything has been going awesome so far, despite the awestruck reactions to my presence by the recruits, and getting drunk, or having anything to drink for that matter, is not on my agenda.

We change in the dorms before hitting up Alberto's. My clothing options are limited for a night out, but I pair my red jeans with a black tank and jean jacket, throw on some dangly earrings, and I'm ready to go. Sienna is my official "host" for the night, and while she checks in on me throughout the night, she's resigned to Lexi taking over as my guide. We really hit it off working out, and she's hilarious as we attempt to play pool. We're both terrible, and she's had a few beers, which makes her efforts even more entertaining. She keeps getting distracted when the music changes, claiming every song is her "favorite" as she belts out the lyrics.

Her teammates are clearly fond of her too, and hang out with us by the pool table. Some of the guys' cross team has joined us, but I haven't spotted Ryan. I keep glancing around, wondering when he'll show up. I'm nervous about how he'll act toward me. Will he ignore me again? His teammates know we went to the same high school, and most of them probably know we dated too. So he can't pretend he doesn't know me.

But the next time I glance up to look around, instead of seeing Ryan, it's Clayton Dennison who I find gazing back, watching me intently. He doesn't look away, like most people do when you catch them staring. Instead, he smiles. I glare back at him. *Don't forget Jace's warning, Clayton*, I want to tell him. But he only smiles wider.

"You know Clayton Dennison?" Lexi asks beside me. We've passed the pool cues to others who want to play, and she's standing beside me with a drink in hand. I have a drink too, but it's a diet Coke.

"Not really." I attempt to sound disinterested, but she's watching me closely. "He went to my high school, that's all."

"He's so hot," she says dreamily.

He is attractive, there's no denying it. But when Savannah sidles up next to him, my whole body tenses.

"Hi Pepper." Ryan's voice distracts me and I turn to find him standing beside Lexi. "Hey, Lexi," Ryan greets her as well.

"How's it going, Ryan?" she asks.

"One of the recruits got wasted," he tells us. "None of us gave him alcohol so I'm not sure how he pulled it off."

"Is he acting like an idiot?" Lexi asks.

"Pretty much," Ryan responds, seemingly unsurprised. "He was annoying all day though, thinking he was hot shit, so none of us really care."

"Is he a good runner?" I wonder, curious if his running talent will outweigh his annoyingness.

Ryan glances at me and shrugs. "He's no Pepper Jones, if that's what you mean."

I roll my eyes. "Well, obviously he didn't win Nationals last year because you did," I remind him. There can only be one National Champion. My stomach churns, the knowledge that it probably won't be me again this year making me queasy.

"He didn't even make Nationals, so after acting like a tool all day and especially tonight, his chances of getting a scholarship offer are slim to none." Ryan's eyes lock on me when he says this, and then he nudges Lexi in the shoulder. "How about the girls? Is it a cool group?"

Lexi nods and opens her mouth to say something but is interrupted by Savannah and Clayton, who manage to maneuver themselves into our circle. "Yo!" Clayton fist bumps Ryan. "What's going on, man?"

Savannah appraises us with her cat-like eyes. "I'm surprised Jace isn't here, Pepper," Savannah says, but she's looking at Ryan. What a weird girl.

"The football team must not have recruits this weekend," I tell her. "He's at a house party or something." I can't remember what he told me about his plans anymore, but her mention of my boyfriend puts me on high alert.

"Oh yeah," Clayton says with a nod. "Turner and the football house are hosting something tonight. They only host this one party all fall and it's usually pretty epic. I'm bummed to miss out this year."

"Can't be too epic if all the awesomeness on campus is right here," Lexi says with her charming smile. She's oblivious to the underlying tension in this conversation.

"Good point," Clayton responds. "I like this girl."

Savannah scowls and Lexi booms, "This *girl* has a name. I'm Lexi."

Clayton introduces himself and Savannah, who turns her gaze back at me. It makes me flinch, and I groan internally that I've shown her she does, in fact, intimidate me a little.

"If I were Jace's girlfriend," she says slowly, letting that obnoxious declaration seep in, "I'd want to be at that party. This is the last time this season the football players party hard before they buckle down for the rest of the season. They go wild, and so do the girls. I'm sure the place is swarming with girls."

My hands ball into fists as I attempt to make my face remain neutral. It's incredibly challenging. "I'm not worried." I trust Jace. But what about these crazy girls? She's right. They'll be all over him.

"Why are you such a bitch?" Lexi asks Savannah in a tone that is not at all bitchy. I can't help it. She's so small and cute that the words coming out of her mouth make me burst into laughter. Ryan and Clayton join me a moment later and Lexi rocks back on her heels with a satisfied smirk. Savannah gives us all a disgusted look before storming away, which only makes us laugh harder.

I almost forget that Clayton is an enemy for a moment. He doesn't seem all that threatening when he's laughing hard at a girl who was bitchy to me. Sure, he's a jerk for being so consumed with his status on campus and that shows that underneath his confident air, he's probably insecure. People like Clayton need others' approval, or worship, in order to feel good about themselves. Not Jace. He's got the worship from others, but he doesn't need it, or even want it. He knows who he is, and that's why he's so damn attractive.

We continue chatting with Ryan and Clayton, and others join us. Knowing we're all athletes gives us a sense of camaraderie, and I almost feel like I already belong at UC. Like I'm one of them. But then something strange starts to happen.

At first, the conversations around me begin to sound slurred, and it almost feels like I'm drunk. Sloppy drunk. The ground feels like it's rippling in waves beneath me. Can anyone tell? I keep glancing around, expecting someone on the cross team to look at me in disapproval. But no one is paying attention.

I glance down at my drink. Did the bartender accidentally put rum in this? Did he think I wanted a rum and Coke? Whiskey and Coke? What do people usually drink with Coke? But when I take another sip, it doesn't taste funny. It tastes like soda normally tastes.

Taking a deep breath, I gather myself and walk slowly to the bar, determined not to trip. But my body wavers back and forth, and I grasp onto someone's shoulder, afraid I'll fall.

"Pepper?" The voice is fuzzy, like it's coming from a static radio channel. My head tilts to the side. Clayton Dennison. Why is he calling my name?

I make out the bartender who served me this soda and I attempt to lift my arm to get his attention, but it feels like it weighs a thousand pounds. I glare at my arm. What has happened to it? The bartender is trying to get my attention now. That's weird. My arm wouldn't even lift and now the bartender is snapping his fingers at me. Blinking in confusion, I remember why I'm standing here.

"This drink," I point to my drink, but when I do, the room begins to spin so quickly that I can no longer keep my balance. And then everything goes black.

***

My head hurts so badly that I'm afraid to open my eyes. It's like someone is hitting me on the head with a hammer. Searing pain vibrates through me and it's only the familiar scent of Jace Wilder on my pillow that provides enough reassurance for me to confront the world. Blinking rapidly, I take in my surroundings. A desk, a chair, a glass of water and bottle of Advil on the bedside table.

Groaning, I try to lift my head, but the shooting pain keeps me down.

"Shhh..." his voice says in my ear. He strokes the hair on my temple. "Let me help you up." Jace's strong arms lift me from behind and despite how slowly he eases me into a sitting position, I hiss at the throbbing in my head. He reaches for the pills and hands me three Advil along with a glass of water. I swallow them and stare blankly ahead.

He rubs my back and it isn't long before the memories of last night infiltrate the wall I was momentarily able to put up. And then the lack of memories. Just, *nothing.*

"What happened?" I croak out. Fear has hit me so hard I can hardly feel the pulsing in my head anymore. It's like an avalanche engulfing me. Something horrible happened to me. I completely lost it. Just blacked out in a bar. On my official visit to UC, the college I've wanted to go to my entire life. I'm gasping for air, realizing I may have lost everything. Everything. And I don't even know why. I can't understand it. What the hell happened?

Not everything, I'm reminded, when Jace takes my hands in his and adjusts us so we're facing each other.

"What do you remember?" he asks quietly, like his own voice could hurt me.

I tell him about playing pool with Lexi, talking with Ryan, and then Savannah and Clayton. "Lexi called Savannah out on being a bitch, and then she left."

"Who left?" Jace asks, and I wonder why that's important.

"Savannah. And then we all laughed. She was acting so vicious. It was just funny." My thoughts are still jumbled. "More people came around us and we were all just talking. I think I was having fun. But then things started to change."

I describe how it felt. I'm not exactly familiar with what it's like to be drunk, but that's what I think I felt like. "So I tried to go to the bar to see what was in my drink. Because I thought I'd just been drinking soda..." My voice drifts off.

I try to remember any details from the moment right before I passed out. "It was like a tunnel was sucking me in and everything got farther away. Someone was calling my name. Clayton, I think."

Jace's lack of response confuses me. I expect him to tense at that, but he doesn't.

"What else?" he asks.

"I think a lot of people were watching," I whisper. "Everyone saw. And then I don't remember anything."

Jace's calm demeanor is forced, I know it. He's trying to be the strong one right now. He sees the confusion and fear on my face, and he sighs. "I was walking to Alberto's with Frankie around midnight. I'd had enough of the house party I told you I had to go to. We weren't sure if the football team was invited to the recruit event, since we didn't have any recruits visiting, but I was hoping to catch you there."

Get to the point, Jace, I think. I have to know what happened to me.

"When I saw Dennison walking along the sidewalk, carrying your limp body, I snapped." Jace lowers his eyes, ashamed. "It's all I saw at first. He was walking quickly, like he was in a hurry, and you weren't moving at all. My heart fucking stopped, Pepper, and I reacted."

"What did you do?" I whisper. I hadn't thought of what Jace might have done. The fear inside me ratchets up another notch.

"Nothing," he says quickly, sensing my fear. "Well, I probably charged him like a fucking bull or something, but I don't really remember. Thank God Frankie was there. That dude is strong. I'm sure I wasn't easy to hold back."

He looks up again, stroking his calloused thumb along my cheekbone and shaking his head. "I was drugged, wasn't I?" There's no other explanation. "Do you think it was Clayton?" I ask, wide-eyed and wondering what the hell might have happened if Jace hadn't been there. Oh God.

Jace shakes his head. "I don't know. I was too crazed to see that he was with others. Two girls on the cross team. Lexi and someone else."

"Sienna?"

"Yeah, Sienna. And Ryan." His muscles twitch at that, but he continues. "Once I took in the others, I realized I'd misunderstood what I saw. They were going to take you to the school infirmary. It was closed by then, though."

"Did you take me to the hospital?"

"No, but we still can. We thought about it and I don't know if we made the right decision. We can still go," Jace offers, searching my eyes.

I quickly shake my head, "No, everyone will hear about this if I do."

Jace nods, feeling a bit more reassured that his decision was the right one. "That's what we decided. Lexi swore you didn't drink any alcohol and the others vouched that you were acting completely sober until a couple minutes before you passed out. You were breathing fine and everything so we just monitored you. It was like you were sleeping."

I take in the dark circles under Jace's eyes and realize he has been awake all night, watching me. I know his visible exhaustion isn't just from sleep deprivation. Jace has stayed up all night partying before and never looks this completely drained. He was scared. And fear will suck the energy right out of you.

But through my concern for him, my fear for my own safety and health, and the pounding on my brain, I suddenly realize I'm supposed to be at the recruitment breakfast.

"What time is it?" I ask, alarmed.

"Ten AM, but don't worry, Lexi and Sienna have it taken care of."

His words do not reassure me. I jump out of bed, and stumble around looking for my shoes. "This is so bad. So, so bad," I repeat over and over. I'll never get a scholarship now.

"Pep, Sienna and Lexi told the coaches that you got sick and had to go home. They got you out of Alberto's so fast they didn't think others really noticed who was being carried out."

I hadn't even thought of that. "Are you kidding? Jace, I'm sure everyone saw. I collapsed in the middle of a crowded bar." And as I say it, I remember Savannah looking at me right before it all went black. If she saw, everyone knows. This really couldn't be any worse.

Well, it could be a lot worse, actually. I shudder at that thought. Who did this to me? Why?

"I should just go to the coaches and explain what happened. I mean, it wasn't my fault."

Jace watches me as I slip my shoes on. "That's your decision, Pep, but you might want to talk to Sienna and Lexi first."

"Why?"

"They were really scared how the coaches would react. They think the coaches will flip, Pepper. Not at you," he says patiently, noting my stricken look, "at the team, for letting this happen. You're the most important high school recruit in the country."

"No. I'm not." I can't even run right now. How can he say that?

"You are," Jace says fiercely. "And the coaches will have to report the incident, do an investigation. Word will get around the NCAA that this happened, and it will be real bad for the team. Just think about it before you tell the coaches. I know you, and I know you won't want people scrutinizing you over this."

He's right. If there's an investigation, it could be bad for the UC cross team, and I definitely don't want that. But aside from Sienna and Lexi, Clayton and Ryan were there too. And Frankie. Not to mention Savannah's intimidating stare before I conked burns in my memory. Everyone might find out about this anyway.

The official visit is over, then. Most of the girls fly out after breakfast and a campus tour, which is probably happening as we speak. I can't know if I've ruined any chances at a scholarship offer by failing to show up this morning. I'm already a risk to them with my injury, and bailing on an official visit can't be looked at lightly, even with an excuse.

And as far as what happened to me last night? "What do we do now?" I ask Jace.

Judging by the look on his face, he's determined to find out who did this. "For now, we wait."

I'm going to need a lot of patience.

After Jace drops me off at home, I send an email to the UC coaches and spend the rest of the day doing homework. Several projects are due in my classes this week, and, while they require most of my attention, the reality of what happened to me is fresh in my mind. It's a darkness that hovers, threatening and taunting me with the possibilities of what it means, and how much worse the night could have gone.

I've turned off my phone in order to help concentrate on my school work, so when Wes arrives to pick me up for dinner, I'm taken by surprise. I completely forgot we were meeting Annie and Jace at Lou's tonight. We made the plans days ago.

The restaurant is packed, as it usually is, when we arrive. Annie and Jace are already there, hanging outside while they wait for a table. It's been a few weeks since I've seen Annie, and I'm taken by her put-together appearance. She's wearing a simple outfit – dark jeans, cotton tee shirt, and a stylish leather jacket. She holds herself confidently, like she's finally figured out who she is. Like she's comfortable with it. A librarian, a mom, and a recovering drug addict.

And Jace's eager expression as we approach tells me he's proud to call her his mother. A lot of sons would be too ashamed of a past like Annie's to bring her around friends, but Jace doesn't dwell on her past. I wonder if it has anything to do with the fact that he's made mistakes too. Jace and his mom aren't letting what they've done in the past define them any longer, and I think they rely on strength from each other to do that.

We've only had a chance to say a quick hello when we're interrupted by Kayla Chambers.

"Hi guys," she says nervously. "I've got a table for you."

"The hostess said it would be another twenty minutes," Jace says.

Kayla is wearing a black tee shirt with the name of the restaurant displayed in red, and a small server apron is tied around her hips. She shrugs. "You got bumped up. Come on in." She gestures for us to follow and we do.

"You still work here?" I ask, after we're all seated.

"I just fill in when they need me. One of the waiters was sick and they called me in."

She stands there awkwardly for a moment, and I wonder if she's our server. The place is swarming with people, so she probably doesn't have time to stay and chat. I catch her eyeing Annie curiously before she rubs her hands together and lets out a deep sigh.

"Listen." She clears her throat. "I've been wanting to apologize for how I acted at the Theta Kapp party a few weeks ago."

Jace and I glance at each other before looking back at Kayla.

"This probably isn't the best time," she notes, gesturing to Annie and Wes, "but I want you two to know that I still have your backs. I'm here for you."

Though she looks earnest, I'm not sure I trust her. It sure seems like she only wants to use her connection to Jace to further her own social agenda, and I don't like it.

"Okay, thanks for the apology, I guess," Jace says dismissively. He doesn't trust her either.

She's going to have to use more than words to show that she's a true friend. When Kayla turns to return to her tables, Annie asks, "What was that all about?"

I expect Jace to shrug it off, like he tends to do with questions he doesn't feel like answering, but he surprises me. "Kayla was a friend of ours at Brockton Public and she goes to UC now. She was bitchy at a party the other night."

"It didn't sound like you accepted her apology," Annie comments.

"I don't," Jace agrees. "She's pledging with a sorority and wanted to flaunt her friendship with me in order to gain their approval. When I didn't take her bait to schmooze with the sorority girls, she pretty much said I'm no fun anymore since I've been with Pepper. That's not an insult I'll forget anytime soon."

"What do you think, Pepper?" Annie asks me.

"About Jace being no fun?" I ask, unsure what she's looking for.

"About Kayla."

"It'd be nice to have more allies, like she says she is, but I'm afraid her true colors came out when she took that dig at me. And Jace. But I think it was mostly at me."

"It was at both of us," Jace clarifies, squeezing on my thigh in reassurance.

"Yeah," Wes chimes in. "Sorority girls always have an agenda. Kayla wasn't the lead girl at Brockton Public because she's soft and sweet. The girl's a user." He glances at Annie before adding, "Not with drugs, though maybe that too, but I mean a social user. All social-climbers need ladders."

"That's deep, man," Jace says, patting Wes on the back with a chuckle. We're interrupted by our waiter, who takes our drink orders. The mood at the table shifts to a more jovial one after that, and it's a good feeling, like all four of us are family. It's still a little weird, not totally natural like it is with just me, Wes and Jace, or with Gran or Jim, but we're getting there with Annie. It's something none of us could have imagined a year ago.

And for that, I'm grateful. Someone is out to mess with me, I was drugged last night, and I can't run right now, but I've got a pretty awesome family. An unconventional one, to be sure, but I'll take it.

Chapter 19

When the University of Oregon offers me a full athletic scholarship two weeks later, the reality of the situation really hits home. If UC doesn't make the same offer, I will have to make a decision. Until Saturday night, my decision would still have been UC, even if they made no offer. But things have changed. I'm sitting on the bus on the way back from a cross country meet that I didn't race. We're an hour away from Brockton, but I'm still haunted.

I don't look forward to my morning workouts at the UC gym anymore. It's usually still dark out when I arrive, and I find myself looking over my shoulder the whole time, wondering when my attacker will show themselves. Because that's what happened. Someone attacked me. And I still have no answers. My mind has been reeling with possibilities about who did this and why. When you hear about the kind of drugging that happened to me, it's associated with date rape. Is that what someone intended? My gut tells me no. This wasn't a stranger targeting a high schooler at a college party. This was more intentional than that.

It was most likely done to hurt Jace somehow. As much as I want to say my love for Jace can withstand anything, sometimes I wonder if that's true. Because I'm afraid all the time now. I ride my bike around town like I'm being chased. It feels like I have a target on my back. I simply can't live like this forever.

Zoe is sitting beside me on the bus, and I know she's concerned. I've told her what happened, and Jace has told Wes. But that's it. Gran doesn't know. She'd call the police for sure. Gran and everyone else believe I'm acting withdrawn because I miss running. And they're

189

not entirely wrong about that. I want to run more than anything.

Patience.

It's a word I chant to myself a lot these days.

Zoe and Wes drag me to Jace's football game that night. I should be happy to support my boyfriend and cheer him on, but going on campus makes me uneasy. Fear has taken root in me, and with it, anger. I'm angry that I'm fearful. If I knew who was after me, I'd face them head on. But I don't. And that gives him an advantage.

Jace has to talk to the press after the game, so the three of us hit up a burger joint while we wait for him to shower. The team no longer pressures Jace to go out with them, as everyone is taking it easy until the end of the season. The playoffs start soon, and UC has a chance to make it to the championship for the first time in years.

"So, what's going on with you two?" I ask Wes and Zoe before taking a huge bite of my burger. It's been three weeks since they first hooked up, and it's time to put Wes on the spot. Besides, I want to take my mind off my own problems.

But Wes doesn't take the bait. "What do you think?" he asks playfully, with his eyebrows waggling suggestively.

Zoe smiles, but she can't hide her disappointment from me. "Can we talk about what happened now?" Zoe turns the tables around, clearly unhappy with my attempt to interrogate them.

"What happened?" I choke out. I know exactly what she's talking about, but I really don't want to go there. I told her only the bare bones of that night, and neither of us have mentioned it since. I don't know what Jace told Wes, but no one has brought it up.

"We can't ignore it," Zoe says urgently. "This is serious, Pepper. We have to find out who it was who did that."

"It could have been anyone," I murmur, placing my burger aside. I've lost my appetite. "It could have been a mistake, for all we know." I look her in the eye. "It might have been meant for someone else."

Zoe narrows her eyes and Wes clears his throat. "Don't lie to yourself, Pepper," Wes says softly. "Let's go over who could have done this. Ryan and Dennison were there, right?"

"Yeah, but they both helped me," I point out.

Zoe isn't convinced. "They might not have expected anything to happen so fast. Maybe they meant to get you alone before it set in."

"You sound like a cop's daughter," I say angrily. Zoe's father is a Brockton cop and it's not something I'll be forgetting any time soon. But this is my life. Not some mystery for her to solve.

"Pepper." Wes's voice is serious now, and he places a hand on mine. It's shaking, and I didn't even realize. "We need to figure out who did this."

My head shoots up. "You don't think I haven't spent every minute going over the possibilities?" I grit out. "We can't know anything for certain, okay? Not until he makes his next move." The last sentence is said quietly, and eerie silence takes ahold of us. They know I'm right. There's nothing we can do. Jace has gone back to the flower shop, telling them this is a potential stalking situation, but they claim they no longer have the records. Without a search warrant, we can't force a flower shop to do a thing. Jace doesn't talk to me about it, but I know he's interrogated everyone who was with me that night at Alberto's. Probably the bartender too.

The weight of everything begins to suffocate me. My life is slipping from my grasp. My goals for this season have gone out the window. The guaranteed scholarship I thought I had to UC disappeared with them. And Jace? If living with a target on my back is what it takes to be with him, I don't know if I can survive like that. But living without him at my side makes my whole body ache in acute sadness just thinking about it.

"I gotta get out of here," I mumble as my breathing becomes erratic. It feels like I'm suffocating. Drowning. I push back my chair, and rush out of the restaurant, barely registering Zoe and Wes's stricken expressions. With no way of getting home beside my own two legs, my body begins to move in the only way it knows how when I'm losing my mind like this. I run.

My legs have a life of their own as they carry me with a vengeance for several blocks, until it registers where I am and what I'm wearing. Converse sneakers and jeans. It's not very comfortable running attire. But my shins don't hurt one bit, and that is a small comfort as I crumple onto a park bench. What the hell am I going to do?

The sound of footsteps makes me whip my head up, the familiar fear surfacing. But it's not my attacker. Jace Wilder's green eyes are burning, but his features soften as he crouches in front of me. His hair is wet from a shower and his cheeks are still flushed from the game.

"You're killing me, Pepper Jones," he says in a near-whisper.

All the feelings swarming inside of me, making me feel crazy, are reflected back at me through Jace. He wants to take it away from me and he can't. That's hurting him more than anything.

"Tell me what to do to make this better," he pleads.

But I'm as lost as he is. I need the x-rays to show my fractures are healed. I need UC to offer me a full scholarship. Whoever is after me needs to reveal themselves. But even then, will this fear go away? Will there always be someone after me if I stay with Jace?

Finally, I decide that he is enough for now. For this moment. "Just hold me," I say simply.

He scoops me up and I curl into his lap, breathing in his familiar post-game scent. The body wash that smells like pine mixed with the clean laundry scent emanating from his hoodie.

"I got an offer for a full scholarship to Oregon this morning," I mumble into his chest. Maybe if my voice is muffled, the blow won't hit so hard.

But he's heard me loud and clear. His body stiffens.

"What?" he says through gritted teeth.

I'm not going to repeat it. "I still haven't heard from UC," I add.

"The coaches never emailed you back?" He's referring to the email I sent the day after the incident, explaining why I ditched the last day of the official visit. I told them it was a stomach virus.

"No, they responded to that. That wasn't a big deal." At least, the email the assistant coach sent me made it *sound* like it wasn't a big deal that I left the visit early.

"Have they made other offers?" he asks, his body still rigid.

"I don't know," I admit. If Ryan and I still spoke, he might be able to give me the inside scoop. But scholarship offers can be complicated decisions, and the athletes on the team are rarely involved in the process.

Jace stands up, keeping me close to his chest. "Just so you know, I'll probably transfer to Oregon if you go there," he says light-heartedly, and I can't tell if he's teasing or serious. Would he really follow me there? Would I want that? Of course I would. Maybe it would be different there. Maybe he wouldn't be such a celebrity.

His Jeep is parked nearby. He must have seen me running like a crazy person and pulled over. "Pepper?" he asks, the seriousness returning again when we're both buckled in.

"Yeah?" I turn to face him.

"It's all going to be okay." He's looking into me, trying to make it right with his words.

"Yeah," I breathe out, "it will be."

Jace hasn't shown me any cracks in his confidence, but my own is beginning to shatter. I'm trying to hold onto him through this, hoping he can have enough for the both of us. He is Jace Wilder after all.

***

I'm gripping Jace's hand with all my newfound upper body strength as we wait for the doctor. It's been five weeks since I last saw Dr. Kennedy in this office, and today I'll find out if the hope I've been grasping onto was in vain or not. If my shins are healing, she might give me the green light to start running again in a week, which means there's still a shot – a long one – at going back to Nationals. Any more than one week of rest, and I'll miss the qualifying meets, not to mention that there simply won't be enough time to get in shape.

Okay, so I'm definitely in shape. With all the weight lifting, core exercises, and pool running I've been doing, my all-around fitness level is amazing. I have muscles I've never had before. But running can't be duplicated in water or on machines. And no matter what I hear today, getting my running legs where they need to be in order to qualify, and then have a chance to actually win – well, some might say I'm crazy to even try.

Not Jace. Sure, he doesn't know running like I do, but his faith in me has been unwavering. When I admitted my wariness about training on campus by myself, he found ways to come with me to work out or have a friend join me. As I opened up to Jace about how seriously the recruit visit incident affected me, I realized it made me feel better. It was like I gave Jace some of my fear and hurt by telling him.

He encouraged me to talk to Zoe about it too, and she's sacrificed some of her late night sneak-outs to go to bed early so she can lift weights with me before classes. It helps having company. The constant fear has lessened, but I still wonder when someone's going to pop out from the bushes (literally and figuratively) to get me.

"Well, Pepper, I have some very good news." Dr. Kennedy is grinning when she opens the door. It's all I can do not to jump up and hug her from that statement, even though she hasn't even relayed the news yet. "Your shins have healed beautifully."

"Really?!" I squeak.

Jace has shifted to the edge of his seat with me. Dr. Kennedy glances between us in amusement. "Hi, you must be Mr. Wilder," Dr. Kennedy introduces herself before delving into an explanation of the x-rays.

When she tells me that I don't even have to wait another week, that I can start running tomorrow, I actually do get up and hug her. She laughs, taken aback.

"It's all your doing, Pepper," she tells me. "A lot of athletes don't listen. They don't rest properly and they end up fighting the same injury for months or years until it becomes a constant reoccurring issue. But yours look great."

I beam, openly pleased that my patience in this particular aspect of my life has paid off.

"But don't get carried away," she warns sternly. "You will be starting out very *slowly* here. I'll be emailing Coach Tom and your trainer my recommendations. It will start out with hardly any running and gradually build up."

"But what about Nationals?" I ask, my happiness dimming. We've discussed the qualifying process and the urgency of my recovery.

196

"You'll be able to go to the State meet, but you'll just have to be comfortable without doing anything too rigorous before the competition," she says like it's obvious.

She doesn't understand. I have to be able to do at least a couple tough workouts in preparation. I'm shaking my head, but Jace places his hand on my knee.

"Pep, you'll be fine. You're going to qualify. Just because you haven't been running doesn't mean you're not fit as hell," he says with such conviction that I'm inclined to believe him.

Dr. Kennedy is nodding in agreement. "He's right."

"I'll do what I need to do," I concede, acknowledging that Dr. Kennedy hasn't let me down yet. I'll be back out running tomorrow. Tomorrow! And whether my goals are lost or not, that is enough for me right now.

Chapter 20

The first run back is both incredible and incredibly depressing. I join the team for a two mile warm-up run and then I'm done for the day. While my teammates do hill sprint intervals, I sit in the training room icing my shins. Just as a precaution. They didn't hurt at all during the jog and it made me realize just how unfamiliar running without pain had become. Running itself isn't something that will ever feel unnatural to me, but I'd become accustomed over the summer to running on tired legs and then to running with shooting pain. It was liberating to run on fresh legs today.

So, despite how short and uneventful the run was, a smile remains glued to my face when I return to my apartment after practice. I'm caught off guard when I find Gran applying lipstick by the hallway mirror.

"Looking good, old lady." She's dolled up, wearing a polka-dotted dress, red Mary Janes, and a variety of bows in her hair. "You got a date or something?"

I'm only half-kidding. Lately, Gran has been mentioning men more often than usual, and with a lot more interest. Gran has been on her own since Gramps passed away a long time ago, and the idea of her going on a date is disturbing, to say the least.

So when she grins brightly at me and rocks back on her heels, I groan. "Seriously?"

"His name is Elmer," she tells me in a giddy voice that I've never heard from her before.

"Like the glue?" I ask. But she ignores me.

"We met at Shirley Dupont's memorial service last week." She clasps her hands and sighs dreamily. "He's a real charmer."

"You met at a funeral? How old is this Elmer?"

She frowns thoughtfully. "Elmer might not be around for too much longer. He has a walker, and his arthritis really slows him down. But he's real lively in spirit!"

Gran never ceases to amaze me. If she wants to go on a date with Elmer, I'm not going to stop her.

"Where are you going?"

"I suggested bowling, but I'm not sure he's got the physical stamina for it, so we're meeting at his assisted living cafeteria."

"You're going on a date at his nursing home?" I clarify.

"Oh, yes. The buffet is wonderful. Lots of soft foods. Easy on the digestion."

"You've been there before?"

Gran gives me a smug look. "Lulu and I sometimes sneak in when you're not around for dinner." And then she cups her mouth like she's telling me a secret, and loud-whispers, "To check out the men."

This is too much. Even for Gran.

"Should I be concerned about you two?" Lulu and Gran on the prowl for men in nursing homes is probably trouble in the making.

"Oh no, dear. Those men couldn't hurt a fly."

"The men aren't who I'm concerned about, Gran, and you know it."

She winks and gives me a brief kiss. "Sorry I'll miss dinner. There's lasagna in the oven for you."

Shaking my head as Gran bustles out the door, I eagerly eat some of the lasagna before saving the remainder in the fridge. It hasn't been easy keeping Gran in the dark about what happened to me at Alberto's. Gran usually knows about everything important that happens in my life. But as I've gotten older, I've learned that some things she's better off not knowing. In this instance, she'll only worry, and that won't make anyone happy.

It's amazing that I'm still feeling the high from my measly two-mile run as I bike to Jace's dorm room later that night. It's dark out and I have a helmet and a bike light now, but the unease hasn't entirely gone away. It's been long enough that I'm starting to think maybe the drugging was random or a mistake. But deep down, something tells me to keep watching my back.

The thrill of running again helps me let my guard down as I turn onto Jace's street. With the anticipation of seeing him, I'm entirely oblivious to the car behind me until the roar of the engine is so loud it's almost on top of me. But it's too late to steer away. I'm rammed from behind and catapulted off my bike. The world spins when my body is launched into the air, over the handlebars, and onto the pavement. Foolishly attempting to break my fall, a loud snap accompanies excruciating pain in my wrist as my body crashes with a force so strong the wind is knocked out of me.

The world swirls, flashing from black to color. The shock keeps me blinking and gasping for several minutes before the pain in my wrist brings me back. A strange cry leaves my lips as I reach for it and curl up in a ball, rocking back and forth. This is it. The attack I knew was coming. Through the haze of pain I realize I need to look around me. The sound of squealing tires forces me to raise my head, and I fight nausea as I catch the tail lights of a white SUV speeding away.

A loud scream of frustration tears out of me and I can hardly believe the noise is from me. Another attack. And still no answers. Only that the person drives a white SUV. The hot tears streaming down my face aren't just from the pain, but from the utter sense of helplessness. Whoever did this is crazy.

Slowly, ever so slowly, I begin to raise myself to my feet. My wrist is throbbing and the rest of my body aches from the impact. The realization that I may not be able to keep running hits me, and the force of that pain sends me right back to my knees. *No.* The pain at the thought that I might be out for the season, for real this time, goes straight to my core. My stomach and my heart feel like they are being ripped right out of me. But I grit my teeth and bite back a new round of tears that threaten.

Whoever did this to me will not have the satisfaction of ruining my dreams. I don't care what the doctors say. I was patient for five weeks. I did everything I was supposed to do. My shins are better. No matter how many cuts and bruises are on my body, I'm running at the State meet next Saturday.

Headlights turn onto the street, and as they race toward me, panic surges through me. I'm in the middle of the road. My body freezes as the car gets closer, and I simply cannot leap into action. This is it. I'm going to be obliterated. The thought hits me, but it's like it's happening to someone else. It doesn't feel real. None of what is happening or just happened seems real.

The car screeches to a stop in front of my bike and the driver and passenger hop out. Two guys in baseball caps and workout clothes race toward me. As one crouches in front of me, I blink in shock. That can't be Clayton Dennison. Why is he always here when something happens? His face is white, reflecting my own shock. He shouts something to the other guy, but I'm not listening. A hysterical sound rips out of me. It's a mix of laughter and a sob.

Clayton is looking around frantically and asking me questions but I just keep shaking my head. His voice is like a buzzing sound in my head. Stars dance in my vision. The thought that this is not real hits me again. And then strong hands are lifting me and I smell pine and clean boy. My vision begins to clear and I burrow into Jace. A dull buzzing continues to follow me as he places me in a vehicle and drives to the hospital. I'm vaguely aware that Clayton and his friend are behind us as Jace talks to the front desk. I'm still in his arms. Why is he carrying me?

"Why are you carrying me?" I ask, and the buzzing begins to fade.

Jace's tense clutch around me eases a bit and he watches me as he slowly lowers me to my feet. He holds me steady and brings his forehead to mine, ignoring the curious receptionist and the others in the waiting room.

His eyes tighten and the pain in his eyes sends a renewed jolt through me. "You were in shock, I think," he chokes out. It almost looks like he's going to break down, right here with an audience, but he pulls himself together.

A police officer approaches us. "Good evening," he says, nodding formally at us, and we break apart to look at him.

"These young men here have informed me that they found you on the road and it appeared you'd been hit by a car," the officer states.

Clayton and his friend stand off to the side with grim expressions.

I simply nod in acknowledgement.

"I'd like to ask you what happened as soon as possible, while it's still fresh in your mind. May I speak with you while you wait to see a doctor?"

Jace swings his head to the receptionist. "Will there be a long wait?" he asks in a dark tone that I can only construe as mildly threatening. Jace can be a little scary when he wants to be.

"No, Mr. Wilder. Only a few minutes." The receptionist knows who Jace is, and I'm not all that surprised. She must be a football fan.

"She was in shock, officer," Jace explains, and I'm grateful he's taking charge right now. I can't even process that this is all really happening. "But I do think she needs to fill you in on what happened." Jace gives me a knowing nod. "On everything that's happened," he adds.

My eyes widen in realization. He thinks I should tell the officer about the drugging and the flowers. And what else? Oh, the same white SUV (I think) that followed me the other night. It all floods at me, and I realize it is more than time to disclose what has been going on. Why did I wait so long, anyway? Right, because there simply wasn't enough information to get anywhere, and I didn't want any publicity.

I gulp. Will *this* be public? Somehow, word about me passing out on the recruit trip never got out. I'm not sure things will stay that way now. With Clayton Dennison and Jace Wilder both in the waiting room of the Brockton ER, news is bound to travel. Fast.

The officer brings me to a secluded hallway and asks me to recall every detail before and after I was hit. I do. And then I tell him about the white SUV that I thought was following me weeks ago. The incident at Alberto's. The flower delivery. The officer is scribbling notes furiously, and he's unable to keep an alarmed expression from his features as I continue to speak.

Jace pops his head in to tell me they are ready to see me, and the officer nods. Expecting Jace to join me, I take his hand, but the officer calls Jace aside. "I need to ask you some questions as well, Mr. Wilder." Jace nods and kisses me on the cheek.

"I'll be waiting right here for you," he murmurs.

I can feel eyes on me as I walk through the waiting room to the nurse, who greets me, "Pepper Jones?"

"Yeah, that's me."

"Come on back."

Twenty minutes later I'm sitting in front of a doctor who is pointing to an x-ray of my wrist. It seems like yesterday... oh, it *was* yesterday... that I was in another doctor's office looking at x-rays. It's broken. The timing couldn't be worse. But maybe that's the point. Who did this?

My dejection must be evident when I return to the waiting room, because Jace leaps from his seat to be at my side. Gran is there too, and I wonder how much Jace has told her. Clayton and his friend have left, and I know at some point I will have to thank them.

Until tonight, I remained suspicious of Clayton Dennison. I never thanked him for helping me at Alberto's because in my mind, he was a prime suspect. But it sure doesn't seem like he is anymore. Jace will hate being indebted to Clayton. But that's the least of our worries right now.

I hold up my wrist, showing him the cast. "Broken," I tell him.

"Can you still run?" he asks. I love that it's his first question. It was my first question to the doctor too. And despite everything that has happened, I find myself grinning stupidly.

"Yes. I can still run."

Gran has jumped up from her seat too, and at this news she breaks into a little boogie. The receptionist claps and the two others in the waiting room smile in amusement. As long as I can still run, nothing else really matters.

Cringing, I admit, "The doctor recommended waiting until my body healed. I'm pretty bruised," I admit. Jace's eyes darken in anger. "But I grilled him and he relented and said that technically, it wouldn't do any serious damage to run with bruising, it just might not be very comfortable."

Jace raises his eyebrows, unconvinced by this reasoning.

"I can handle bruises, Jace."

He doesn't argue, knowing now is not the time. I'm putting on my fiercest, most determined look, and I'm prepared to fight anyone who tries to talk me out of running.

"You're a tough girl. You can take it." The emotion in his voice melts me. And even though Gran is watching, he tugs me to him for a kiss. A serious one. His tongue caresses mine, and all I want is for him to take me away.

Gran must know what I'm thinking. "Pepper," she interrupts us. "Where do you want to go tonight?"

Her understanding means more to me than I can say. Jace isn't just a boyfriend. He's my family. So is Gran. But I need Jace tonight. And Gran's acceptance of that fact warms me. She loves Jace too, and she knows he'll take care of me.

Jace is waiting patiently for me answer. "I'll stay with Jace tonight," I say.

His relief is evident and Gran nods before hugging us both and heading out. She's already taken all the medical forms from me and I'm sure will head straight to the store in the morning to get everything I need for my wrist.

"Did you tell her?" I ask Jace.

"Not everything. That's for you to do," he says.

"I kind of wish you had already. I'm not looking forward to breaking the news to her." She'll be devastated someone is after me and terrified as well. I wonder if she'll even let me continue to go on campus.

"Let's talk about it all tomorrow. Tonight, we're going to Shadow Lane."

I don't realize how tense I am about returning to campus until he says this, and I'm filled with relief.

He takes my hand and leads me to the parking lot. "You're having a bubble bath and a glass of wine."

Something about the way Jace says bubble makes me giggle. "Does the Wilder household even have bubbles for a bath?" I ask skeptically.

He scoffs. "We've got what we need."

"And after the bath?" I wonder out loud. A different kind of tingle takes ahold of me now. A delicious one.

He shoots me a dark glare before opening my door and helping me in. "Bed. Lots of sleep. You aren't going to classes in the morning. And neither am I."

"But Jace, you can't skip class," I protest, ignoring the other part of his statement for the moment. It's important that he remain in good standing with his courses.

"This incident is enough to warrant a valid absence. And if it's not, fuck it. We're staying in bed tomorrow morning."

When he tucks me in later that night and I'm snuggled close to his warm, firm body, I feel safe and protected. But as I drift off, it dawns on me that in all likelihood, the person driving that car tonight was after me because of what I mean to Jace. How can Jace make me feel safe if he is the reason I'm being attacked? I don't know that for certain, but the irony of the situation presses on me as I burrow into Jace's body. He can't help who he is, what he means to people. But I can help what he means to me, if I want. My aching body distracts me from resolving the troublesome thought and I drift into a deep sleep.

Chapter 21

The possibility that I might not get to compete at State for a different reason – one entirely out of my control – doesn't really hit me until Friday evening. Rollie's parents hosted a pre-race pasta dinner the night before the District Championships. The girls' team has to place first or second overall to qualify as a team. Only ten teams in Colorado qualify for State as a team; everyone else has to qualify individually. In the past, I've qualified individually and last year we also qualified as a team. Since I'm not racing and can't qualify individually, the only way for me to get to State is if the whole team qualifies. I'd been so concerned with my own recovery, I hadn't even thought that the team might not place first or second.

I barely sleep the night before Districts and I've never been so nervous for a race in my life. One I'm not even competing in. I've been running a couple of miles each day all week, even with the cast on my wrist. My body certainly felt off the first couple of days after the accident, but my shins didn't hurt, and my wrist didn't really hold me back. It made me feel a little less streamlined and slightly off-balance, but I could still run. And so I did.

I've warmed up with the team, and today I get to cool down with them too, but I'm relegated to the sideline for the race. Though there are plenty of parents, siblings, friends, and even some of my teammates who aren't racing today either (each school can only race twelve people at this meet), I prefer to be alone for this. I'm wound tight with anticipation.

We won Districts last year, but my freshman and sophomore year we placed third, and didn't qualify as a team. Without me racing, our odds of placing first or second are low. If everyone has a great day, it can happen, but it's far from guaranteed. How I had avoided facing this reality until now is extraordinary. Perhaps I needed to hold on to some hope, any hope, that my goal remained attainable. I had to believe I could race at State in order to get through the cross training. Otherwise, the hopelessness of the situation would have been too much.

The first crowd of runners is coming my way. I hear them before I see them. I'm away from most of the other spectators, about a half mile in to the course. Most of the runners are still pretty close together, and I shade my eyes, trying to make out the blue and gold colors of Brockton Public. Jenny's tiny frame is out in front, and my mouth curves into a small smile.

When I collapsed at State last year and missed qualifying for Regionals by one spot, Jenny gave up her spot for me. Judging by the look of determination on her face as she races along with girls I recognize as the top competitors in our District, I know she's not just racing for herself today.

Over the last couple of weeks, Zoe has focused on cross with a renewed vigor, apparently recognizing this season likely will be her last ever. She's realized she doesn't have the commitment to the sport to continue in college. And Zoe is right there, on the heels of the top group. She flashes me a smile when she sees me and I cheer loudly.

It's the top five girls on each team who score points, with six and seven only counting if there's a tie. Though our other runners aren't super strong, they consistently place in the middle of the pack. They will need to do better than that today.

I cheer with a ferocity that probably scares some of the runners, but I don't care. I'm all over the course, probably running more than I'm supposed to in order to get to each spot to cheer, but I'll sit out the cool down if I need to.

Jenny is battling two girls who are twice her size when she hits the home stretch. I can see her digging deep, seeking that *something else* inside her that not everyone can find. She's a true competitor, and when her stride begins to surge, I know she's got what it takes. The two other girls (who are certainly not big by any means, but who appear as giants compared to Jenny), notice that Jenny is pulling ahead. They pump their arms harder but they can't hold on. And when she crosses the finish line in front of them, I'm the first to embrace her.

Zoe joins us a moment later, having placed higher than ever before at the District meet. More girls from our team filter across the finish line, until we're squeezed to the side in a group circle. They are sweaty and dirty and the joy on all of their faces, knowing they've raced their hardest, brings tears to my eyes.

These girls did their best and they know it. I'm incredibly proud to be their teammate, their captain. Whether we make the cut for State or not, I'll be okay. We'll all be okay.

Though I'm at peace with whatever happens, waiting for the results to come through is a new test in patience. The boys' team is strong enough this year to be quite confident they either won or at least placed second.

They'll be at State. But the rest of us can't stop fidgeting as we sit on the grass attempting to talk about plans for the night. We're all too distracted to pay much attention to the conversation, yet we keep talking anyway. Nerves will do that.

The guys have declared a celebration either way, especially once I told Omar and Rollie – the boys' captains – that the girls raced awesome today, no matter what place they end up getting.

Coach Tom is running toward us and I jump up from my cross-legged position. Coach often jogs around the course at races and even occasionally at practice to help motivate us. But the pep in his gait tells me all I need to know and I'm grinning before he even announces the news.

We're going to State. The dream is still alive.

***

"We're going to State!" Zoe chants for the hundredth time. She's drunk. And very excited for the State meet.

We're standing around a campfire about a mile from anywhere else. It's a campsite that has been closed for the season, but given that it's the cross country team, we hiked a mile in with beer in backpacks. Our cars are parked where a gate blocks the road, and we know the odds of anyone checking things out is slim to none.

It was Omar's idea, and I love it. It's cold out, and we're bundled in parkas and hats, but this is just the cross team tonight, and the celebratory vibe in the air is contagious. Even though I didn't participate in getting us to the State meet, I feel a part of it.

I'm holding on to a thermos of hot chocolate and watching the fire, glad that enough of us aren't drinking so we can get all the cars back, when I jump at arms wrapping around my waist. Though they are strong and familiar, I have to spin around to confirm it's him.

"Jace," I breathe out. "What? How did you get here?"

He laughs. "How do you think? We parked where the road closed and walked the rest of the way."

"We?" I frown, looking around.

"Me and Wes," he tells me. "Omar told me what you guys were up to tonight so I decided to surprise you."

My expression must not be what he hoped for because he loosens his hold a bit.

"I know it's supposed to be just the team and everything, but Omar said you guys have been here since eight or so, and I figured people would be heading back soon," he explains. He's right. It's nearly midnight and a lot of people have curfews.

"No, I'm glad you're here, just surprised," I tell him. It's true. His warmth feels good. But there's tension between us. I haven't seen him since Tuesday morning, the morning after I was hit by the car. I'm not sure who has been avoiding whom, but there's definitely a distance between us.

He knows these things are probably happening to me – terrible things – because I'm with him. I know it too. And neither of us knows what to do about it. We aren't giving up. Whoever is doing this wants to hurt us, and as much as neither of us wants to admit it, they've succeeded. We can't ignore what's going on.

"Can I talk you into spending the night?" Jace murmurs. I've twisted back around to face the fire. It's a welcome distraction. I love being in his arms, but I don't want to talk right now.

"You don't have to talk me into it, Jace." I tilt my head back to tell him and he takes my lips in a brief kiss. But that kiss tells me so much. Jace holds me and touches me in a way that communicates he's still deeply in love with me, and probably always will be. But how do we handle whoever wants to hurt him by hurting me? Can we fake a breakup and stay together secretly? The only solutions I've contemplated over the past few days are simply too extreme. Too heartbreaking.

When I break my eyes from his I see that Wes is by Zoe, who is even happier than she was earlier, which is saying something. Our teammates don't hide their amazement that Wesley Jamison and Jace Wilder are at our little celebration, and they stare in open fascination. Being a spectacle in front of my own teammates doesn't bother me like it might have a year ago. Instead, I find it amusing. Omar and Rollie are used to Wes and Jace by now, and they are the only ones who don't seem dumbstruck. And maybe Jenny. She's too interested in being seated on Rollie's lap to care.

After making sure everyone's ride home is accounted for, Jace and I make our way back to his Jeep. Though I didn't race, the emotions of the day have taken their toll, and I'm yawning all the way back to Jace's dorm.

He doesn't stop holding my hand. He holds it as we walk to his car and while driving, and all the way up the stairs to his room. "My roommates are out," he tells me as he unlocks the door to his common area, which is generally unlocked.

"I'm just going to run to the restroom real quick. I'll meet you in your room." I kiss him on the cheek as he makes his way to his dorm room and I slip into the bathroom the four boys share.

Despite how sleepy I am, my stomach flutters in anticipation of alone time with Jace as I wash my hands after doing the business I came to do. It's eerily dark and silent in the dorm. Usually at least one of the guys is home, and the building itself is generally full of the sounds of dozens of college students living under one roof. But it's Saturday night, and most of the athletes are either asleep, partying, or away at a game.

After drying my hands with a paper towel, I open the door and glance up to see light coming from Jace's doorway. The door is partially open and Jace is standing there, facing inside, a grim expression on his face. I stop in my tracks when he puts his hand out behind the door, a stern gesture to stay away.

Gulping, I open my mouth to ask what's going on when I hear a girl's voice. My knees begin to quake. It's a voice I know. Savannah, the amazon.

I can't hear what she's saying and very slowly I inch my way closer to the door. Jace tenses when he senses me beside him, but she can't see me. I'm still shadowed by the door. Jace doesn't look at me, and it dawns on me that he wants her to keep talking. He doesn't want me to interrupt her.

When I hear what she's saying, I jump into action. I'm filled with a sense of purpose and I grab my phone from my back pocket, frantically searching for the app that records conversation. My movements are jerky, but with determination I hit the record button. And just in time.

Chapter 22

"The first time I saw you, I knew that you had to be mine," Savannah says in a strangely trance-like voice. "It was two years ago and you were at my high school for a football game. I was leaving the locker room after practice and you almost ran into me in the hallway. You remember that, don't you?"

Jace's face remains carefully expressionless, but she clearly imagines a response because she continues confidently, "I knew you noticed me then. You looked at me like you loved me even then. It was love at first sight," she sighs dreamily and my stomach lurches. "Of course, I'd already heard all about you. I knew who you were. But we couldn't be together then. It wasn't time."

Jace's breathing is steady and if it wasn't for his white-knuckled grip on the doorframe, I might mistake him for calm. His stance is deliberately casual, though he has made no move to step closer to her.

"I've seen the way you look at me. I know you want me too. But your childhood friend is holding you back." She says *childhood friend* like I'm already in the past. Like I'm nothing. Nobody. It's hard not to storm in right there and then. But I know I have to wait. She will admit to everything. I'm sure of it. The crazy in her voice tells me she's responsible for everything.

"It's okay, Jace," and her voice is closer now. A pale hand touches Jace's chest and I inhale sharply. Though every bone in my body wants to slap her hand away, I take a step back. Very slowly.

"You can let her go now. I know you feel a duty to stay with her and I respect that, but it's our time now. She can't fight me. She's pitiful." Her eerie voice turns hard now. Bitter.

"Did you send Pepper the flowers?" Jace asks quietly.

"Don't!" She holds up a hand. "Don't say her name when we're together."

Jace nods, showing no reaction.

"I did." And then she lets out a high-pitched giggle that sends shivers down my spine. "That was just for fun. But the roofies in her soda did not work out how I wanted." She sounds annoyed. "I must have given her too much because Clayton didn't have time to make a move."

"Dennison?" Jace can't hold back the threat in his voice.

"Or Ryan," she says casually. "Or anyone, really. It didn't matter."

Jace is losing patience now. The rapid ticking in his jaw muscles tells me he won't be able to hold it together for long. But we have enough now, even if I stop recording.

"And hitting her on the bike?" he asks softly, in a tone I've never heard from him before. He's trying to show no emotion, but there's a darkness in his depths that is unmistakable. "Was it you driving?"

"What do you think?" And it's a seductive voice from Savannah now. I can hardly keep up. She's all over the place. "She'll stay away now. She hasn't been here all week, has she? She's afraid. I'm the one with the power. And I think you need to be with a powerful woman." Her fingers touch just below his collarbone and run down the length of his chest. "You are a powerful man."

Jace closes his eyes and it almost looks like it's from pleasure. Why doesn't he stop her?

"How did you get in here?" Jace asks, still seeking more information.

There's a pause before Savannah answers, and when she does, she sounds confused. "You left them out for me, don't you remember? It was last week, and you stopped to talk to all of us in the common area before leaving one afternoon. I thought," she hesitates, second-guessing herself, "you gave me a knowing look when you put your keys on the table, and then you never picked them up."

Jace doesn't say anything. The color is beginning to drain from his face as he loses his composure. I do remember him looking for his keys and I ended up giving back the spare pair he had given me when he couldn't find them. Savannah reaches for him again and I suck in a breath. What is he planning to do? He can't communicate with me though. I'm not leaving, if that's what he expects. I want to confront her.

I'm about to do just that when the common area door swings open. Frankie flips on the lights and I notice he is tugging the hand of the soccer girl who was watching him the other night. Not pigtail girl, but one of the two who didn't seem bothered by me being there.

He freezes when he sees Jace standing in his doorway, a hand reaching out from the other side while I hide close by, my phone outstretched.

"Uh, hey guys, what's going on?" Frankie asks hesitantly.

Jace shoves the door open and I can hear Savannah stuttering as she crashes to the ground. I rush to his side, on the offensive, but a laugh of disbelief erupts from my chest when I find Savannah sprawled on the ground. She's wearing the kind of lingerie you might find in a kinky sex store. Not that I've ever been to one, but all I can think is that she looks ridiculous. His room is lit with an array of candles, and rose petals litter every surface.

With her hair wild and askew, her face pale in shock, I can't help but take pity. My reaction startles me. But there's no doubt that this girl is sick. This isn't just a mean girl with a jealous vendetta like Madeline Brescoll. This girl is crazy. Certifiable.

Just as pity sets in and I let my guard down, she launches herself from the floor at me. Her eyes are set on my wrist with the cast, and she reaches for it with a snarl, but only her fingernails touch me, ripping skin from my arms. Jace has already grabbed her and pulled her away. Her arms and legs flail.

Frankie is pulled from his frozen disbelief and rushes toward us.

"Take her, man." Jace shoves Savannah at him, which is no easy feat given her size. "I don't want her near me." Frankie easily handles her. The right guy for the job.

The girl who was with him is already on her phone, and I can hear her talking to campus security. Though I imagine the police will need to be called into this one. When Jace takes me in his arms, pulling me away from the situation, all clear and rational thoughts escape me. I begin to gasp for air and a sob escapes.

He rubs my back and though it brings me some comfort, I'm lost in the utter absurdity of what just happened. A girl obsessed with my boyfriend. Driven crazy by it. *Again.*

Again.

My sobs stop and my breathing begins to return to normal as I process that this is not the first time a girl has been driven to do crazy things over Jace Wilder. Madeline Brescoll's behavior was tame compared to Savannah's, and I can't help but wonder if this will only get worse. It seems impossible and likely at the same time. Jace's celebrity status is bound to continue growing. Will there be more girls like Savannah in the future?

At that thought, my heart turns cold and a strange numbness settles through me. Slowly, I pull out of Jace's arms and take a step back. He watches me closely, his eyes giving away nothing. I can hear Savannah struggling behind us with Frankie, but it doesn't affect me. I don't feel pity or fear anymore. I can't feel anything at all.

Campus officers arrive and the police shortly after that. Savannah is taken away and all four of us are questioned. Frankie and the girl, whose name I learn is Lizzie, are dismissed at some point, but Jace and I remain until the early morning hours. They have the recording, and it seems that should answer all their questions, but they need us to make statements and sign papers. I remain detached throughout the entire process.

Jace asks me where I want to go at some point and I tell him home. If he thinks I'm staying in his dorm room he's nuts. I'm not sure I'll ever stay there again after Savannah contaminated it with rose petals, candles, and... her body. But those thoughts don't make me queasy like they should. I simply feel empty. The idea that I might not go back to Jace's dorm, and what that means, causes a small tug in the pit of my stomach but nothing more. I've completely shut down.

And Jace knows it. He doesn't push. He helps me into bed, and as I fall asleep, I can hear him talking in hushed tones with Gran, who must have heard us coming home. It's a wonder I can sleep at all, but I fall into a long, deep, dreamless state.

I sleep for nearly twenty-four hours. Well, I'm not sleeping the entire time. I can hear people talking in the apartment at several points, but I stay in in bed. The cops have my cell phone, which I handed over so they could take the recording into evidence. I'll get it back in a couple of days. But really, I'm grateful that I'm unreachable right now.

I get up once to use the restroom and brush my teeth late Sunday night. Gran left food on the kitchen table with a note to wake her whenever I want. But I'm not hungry. When I wake early Monday morning, I still have no appetite, but I eat a banana and drink some tea before heading to school.

I'm entirely unprepared for the stares and whispering. Pitying looks, alarmed expressions, they follow me everywhere. But I isolate myself with a hard shell, solidifying myself with numbness. I remain distant even as I talk to Zoe and my teammates about what happened.

At practice, I'm allowed to join the team for part of their speed workout on the track. It feels good, holding nothing back as I sprint around the track a few times, but my emotions remain muffled and dim. My speed is way better than I expected, but there's only a slight glimmer of joy that fizzes out immediately instead of the elation I would expect to follow me for the rest of the week.

Zoe and Gran are concerned, but they don't pry. They just hover all week, checking in frequently and eyeing me closely. Even Annie stops by once. I avoid Jace. And he lets me. The cops return my phone on Tuesday, and he texts me a few times, but when I don't respond, he doesn't show up at the apartment or try calling or anything. I'm not sure if I want him to. I'm not sure how I feel at all.

When the State meet arrives on Saturday, I go through the familiar race day routine like a robot. I eat my usual breakfast, pack my race bag, put my warm-up clothes on over my uniform, tie my hair in a ponytail with two hair ties, and paint my fingernails the school colors. Well, I don't paint my nails for every meet, just the big ones.

I really have no idea what to expect at this race. It's a 5K race and I've only run that distance a couple of times since I recovered from my injury. As for running fast, I've only done the one speed workout, and it was a short one. The team spent this week "tapering" – which means they were taking it easy. For most, this will be the last meet of the season. It might be for me as well, but that thought doesn't bring the shooting pain it would have weeks ago.

It's my competitive spirit that breaks through the hard shell blocking my emotions. I've positioned myself near the front of the pack and I'm embracing the burn in my legs. It's a familiar feeling that I've missed. The pace begins to pick up, and it takes a moment before I realize about a dozen girls are breaking away from the pack. I'm right in the middle. Jenny is beside me, and she begins to pick up her pace in order to stay with the lead group.

I need to place in the top seven to qualify for Regionals. I have to stay with the lead group. But in order to do that, I'm going to have to push hard. My legs are already burning, and the race is only halfway through. After crashing and burning at numerous races as a freshman, I learned to hold back. But I can't do that now. I have no choice. Sure, a few of those girls might crash and I can pick them off later, but that's not a risk I'm willing to take.

So I pump my arms harder and urge myself forward, knowing that my body will be tested like never before. It hasn't run this pace in weeks, and it's protesting the exertion.

Coach Tom shouts words of encouragement as I close the gap with the top group.

"That's it, Pepper, stay right with them. Just stay with them."

I chant that motto over and over as they pick up the pace even more up a hill. Normally I am the fastest up hills. It's when I drop people and pull ahead. But it takes every ounce of energy left inside me to stay with the group as the course takes us up what feels like a never-ending mountain. I'm unaware of anything else, just the importance that I stay with this group. No matter how much my lungs are screaming at me.

Before I know it, girls around me are falling back, unable to maintain the pace as the finish line comes into view. The top group of a dozen begins to break up and I hold on for dear life. It's Jenny's tiny frame that I lock my gaze on, doing everything in my power to stay with her. I glance to each side, counting. Four have pulled twenty feet ahead. Two are on each side of me, and Jenny is just in front of me.

My body fights me as I try to compel it into a different gear. But it takes everything in me just to stay on Jenny's heels. The two girls on the right close in on her, while the other two fade back. Jenny picks it up and I close my eyes as the pain in my body washes over me. I can't let the two girls to my right beat me. Then I'd be in eighth place. Just like last year. And Jenny isn't giving up Regionals for me again. I wouldn't allow it even if she tried.

The finish is 100 feet away but it might as well be 100 miles. My body begins to ease up, relenting to the pain, resigned to the fact that this will be my last cross race for Brockton Public. But I grit my teeth, fighting with my own legs.

No. This isn't it.

The anger at my own momentary willingness to give up fuels me and to my own surprise, I surge forward. I can see the first four girls sprinting through the finish line as I move past Jenny on my left and the two other girls on my right. Jenny matches me stride for stride as we leave the two others behind.

We cross the finish together, and I'm tempted to collapse in exhaustion right there, but Jenny throws an arm around my waist and it keeps me upright. She's small but strong as hell.

We've placed fifth. Jenny and I tied, and we'll be heading to Regionals together. Zoe finishes strong with her best time ever on a cross country course. My happiness oozes out, but I keep it in check. I can't let it all out. If I do, my emotions will cripple me.

So I beg out of another celebration that night. Jenny and I are the only ones on our team who qualified for Regionals, and everyone else wants to party hard in recognition of the end of their season. Even the feeling of duty and obligation to support my teammates can't get me to come out tonight. I claim that I'm getting sick and I don't even feel guilty for lying.

I'm relieved that my season isn't over. That my goals aren't lost. If they were, the hard shell I've built around my emotions would shatter. Instead, I let myself feel a twinge of happy relief that Regionals is coming up next. It's something sure and concrete to work towards. Jace is gone at a game this weekend, and for that I'm relieved as well.

Savannah is on some sort of house arrest in her hometown. She's a five-hour drive from here, and I no longer have a target on my back. But Jace is still a celebrity in the world of Brockton and on campus. And I still have no word from UC about a scholarship. Instead of sorting through what this all means, I'm putting all my energy into qualifying for Nationals at the Regional meet in two weeks. Aside from that, I will think of nothing else. I simply can't.

Chapter 23

My single-minded focus reaps the results I was seeking. I qualify for Nationals at the Regional meet. And so does Jenny. But it's like my emotions have been frozen in ice. Sure, I act happy but again, it's mostly just relief. Relief that I'll continue to have something to focus on for another two weeks. Gran tried to sit me down and talk to me about what's going on. Even she knows that me qualifying for Nationals after being out with an injury for most of the season is a huge hurdle, and that I should be ecstatic. Oh, and not to mention that I'm still wearing a cast for a broken wrist.

When I brush her off with vague answers she takes my hands. "Jace has come by multiple times, and you've acted so cold to him, Pep," she points out. Her view of my behavior threatens a sharp stab of emotions but it disappears immediately. "Girl, you have never been a cold one, and I don't like it. Not one bit. Stop acting like a zombie and tell your Gran what's weighing on you."

I swallow a lump in my throat and shake my head. "I'm okay, Gran, really. I just need some time. And I've told Jace that. He understands and we're okay with that."

"You sure he's okay with it? That boy looks like you've punched him in the gut every time you give him the zombie routine," she says solemnly. "I'm as worried about him as I am about you."

My head shoots up. Something inside me threatens to shake free but I stubbornly push it back down.

"The thing with amazon girl really shook both us up," I say calmly. It's quite the understatement. Gran huffs loudly and even Dave growls from under the table. "Just let me process it. I've got to focus on Nationals right now, okay?"

Gran narrows her eyes. But it's all I've got.

What I learn over the next two weeks is that I am only capable of suppressing my emotions for so long. They can't be dulled forever, and when they start to hit, they are sharper than ever.

Jenny and I are the only ones at practice together, and our workouts are very mild. While she's in taper mode after training hard all season, these workouts are actually building my speed so I don't make a fool of myself at Nationals. I'm not even sure I believe I can win anymore. Who am I kidding?

Jenny chats about her new relationship with Rollie and he picks her up from practice every day. Seeing them together is hard. I can't deny it. I miss Jace. I really miss him. He's tried giving me the distance I've asked for, but I know he's hurting.

When a letter arrives two days before we fly to Indiana for Nationals, offering me a full athletic scholarship to UC, another piece of the wall breaks. Mark Harding leaves me a voicemail, apologizing that the scholarship letters went out later than usual this year due to some board meetings, and that he was anxiously awaiting my decision. But instead of calling him back immediately, I sit on it. Something is holding me back.

And that something is waiting for me in my room when I get back from my last high school cross practice on Thursday evening.

He's sitting at my desk, and the letter is in his hand.

He doesn't look up when I enter or when I sit down on my bed.

"I got it yesterday," I say quietly.

"Yeah, I saw the date." Jace shows no remorse for reading my mail, and I don't expect him to.

For some reason, he can't look at me.

"Pepper." The pain in his voice shatters all my protection. My heart is breaking for him. "I'm sorry. I know I should be the strong one here. I know that being with me has cost you in ways neither of us could have imagined. It's put you in danger. And," he sucks in air like he's struggling to breathe, "I just can't let you go."

"Let me go?" I echo. "Break up with me?"

His eyes finally find mine, and I want more than anything to crawl into his lap and make it all better again.

He swallows. "That would be the right thing to do, wouldn't it? To keep you from the shit that follows me around," he says with some disgust. "After you left that morning. The morning after you were hit, I was so fucking scared you'd end it right then. But you didn't. You came with me that Saturday night. And then..." His voice trails off and neither of us can say a thing.

"And then we found out who was behind it all."

"Yeah," he says on a heavy sigh. "We did."

He gets up from the chair now and joins me on the bed, but he still won't touch me.

"I've been terrified since then that you would end it, but you've checked out. Just put me out of my misery here,

Pepper. I've given you space but I just, I can't stay away."

"Jace, I'm flying to Indiana for Nationals tomorrow." He must know this. It's been all over the news. Oh, and he sent me chocolate-covered strawberries after Regionals to congratulate me. I'm not sure he'll ever be able to send me flowers again.

He blinks. "Yeah, I know." He runs a hand through his hair. "I'm sorry. This is shitty timing."

I can't help but offer a small smile. He's so distraught. It's painful to see him like this. Jace is supposed to be cool, calm and collected at all times. "So you came to tell me that you'll understand if I break up with you because of the crazy you attract?"

I'm trying to sound teasing and light-hearted, but the gravity of the words can't be missed.

He nods slowly.

My eyebrows furrow and I gasp at a sudden realization. "Do you *want* me to break up with you?"

"Fuck, no," Jace practically growls at me. And he finally pulls me to him. His touch eases me in a way I haven't felt soothed in weeks. "I want you to be safe, and if being with me is going to keep making you a target, I'm not sure we've got a choice."

"She's gone now, though." But we both fear the same thing. That there will be more like her.

"I've had no idea what you've been thinking, Pep, and it's driving me crazy."

I push back so I can have enough distance to think. His hard chest and warm breath are entirely too distracting. "Honestly?"

"That's all I want."

"I've been shut down because I'm not sure I can handle being your girlfriend."

His eyes darken at that, but I continue. "I've gotten a lot tougher since we first got together, Jace, but being with you takes a really strong girl. And it's only going to get more intense."

He raises his eyebrows in question.

"Your," I wave my hand around in the air, "fame!" There's already talk of when he'll be drafted to the NFL. My voice softens when I admit, "Savannah was right about one thing. You're powerful. And I can't ignore what that means for me."

His body stiffens at her name, but he asks as gently as he can, "What does it mean?"

I shrug. "Do I have what it takes?"

His lips begin to curve in a smile but I stop him from saying anything yet.

"It's why I shut down. If I feel everything, I might discover I'm not cut out for it. And I don't want to discover that. Does that make me weak?"

Jace shakes his head and I can tell he's been exercising a lot of control not to tug me back to his chest when he finally gives in and presses a hard kiss to my forehead.

"You're the strongest girl I've ever known."

My body shudders at his words, at his conviction that they are truth.

And when he takes my hand, and then my mouth in his, I let myself melt into him. I'm not sure if I ever really had a choice. If being with Jace Wilder requires being strong, I'd better keep training.

***

Gran flies on a plane for the first time in her life to watch me at Nationals. It's the same day as the championship game for football. UC made it for the first time in twelve years. Brockton is going crazy for their quarterback. Jace did me a huge favor by taking some of the attention away from me today. Only one other girl has won Nationals twice in high school, and that's Elsa Blackwood, who went on to win a bronze medal in the Olympic marathon.

The pressure to win again doesn't bother me like it would have in the past. I'm stronger now. I'm confident in who I am as a runner.

Jenny is giddy with nervousness and I don't blame her. I try to be encouraging, but I'm mostly lost in my own anticipation as we warm up and finally toe the line. I've found my racing legs again over the past few weeks, and it's truly astonished me how well I was able to maintain fitness by cross training alone. But whether I'm in the kind of shape to compete with the best in the nation has yet to be seen.

When the gun goes off, for the first time maybe ever, I have no racing plan or strategy. Coach Tom advised going with my gut, whatever that means. He's usually quite conservative in his advice, and I assumed he wanted me to hang in the back so that I could see how much gas I had left at the end to try to finish respectably. To avoid embarrassment. But as the field surges forward and girls try to find their position in the pack, my gut is telling me to go for it.

So I do.

Keeping my elbows out to avoid getting pushed by the other runners surrounding me, I kick my legs hard in order to get to the front. If I get boxed into the middle of the pack before we hit the narrower trail, I'll waste a lot of energy trying to pass people later on.

There are still a number of girls ahead of me when we merge onto the trail, but I'm not as far back as I thought I'd be. As soon as the first hill comes into sight, my heart races in anticipation. Instead of slowing as we incline, I pick up my pace, surging past several runners and making it to the front pack of girls by the time we reach the top.

A couple of them seem startled by my presence beside them as we wind our way through the woods, and I notice one does a double-take. People heard about my injury and assumed I was out of the running. Until the gun went off, I believed it too. I held on to a hope, but I thought I was fooling myself. As the rush from racing with top runners floods through me, I know that we were all wrong.

I am very much in the running.

A grin spreads across my face when I see Coach Tom on the sideline. He wasn't expecting me so soon, and his eyes widen in surprise before he gathers himself and shouts encouragements.

Gran has adorned herself in a hot pink parka and ear muffs today. She wanted me to be able to see her in the crowd. I don't think she realizes I never have trouble spotting her. The tiny woman has vocal chords like a lion when she cheers.

Some girls might be embarrassed to hear their name shouted with such unguarded enthusiasm, but Gran's joy at watching me run always makes me want to run harder. I love that she loves how much I love to run. Yup. I am so feeling the love as I keep up with the lead pack of girls going into the final mile.

It's a cold and cloudy December day, and my body was made to run fast in weather like this. I've gotten used to the cast on my wrist these past few weeks, and it doesn't feel so weighty anymore. It's just there.

The throbbing in my legs and chest becomes more insistent and my own labored breathing mixes with that of the girls around me. But when the finish line comes into view, the goal I've been holding on to so tightly over these past few months becomes a reality. And the throbbing no longer matters anymore.

I focus on that finish line, the movements of hot pink bouncing up and down registering somewhere in my periphery and spurring me to a speed I didn't know I had left in me. The roar of the crowd is deafening but all I can see is the finish.

My arms pump and my knees lift with determination. It dawns on me that there are no runners beside or in front of me but I don't back down. I race for that finish line like my life depends on it. And in an odd way, it's this moment that has gotten me through everything.

Being here, running my heart out, sprinting ahead of everyone else, it's what I live for.

Chapter 24

"Pepper Jones is my hero!!" Zoe screams and swings me around. "Two-time National Champion, baby. Right here in this room!" We're at Wes's house a week after Nationals, and the entire cross team is there, along with Jace and a few of his friends on the football team. Most of my teammates have now had enough to drink that they are no longer staring in shock at Jace and his enormous friends.

"Seriously, I worship you," Zoe tells me before putting me down. "You too, peanut." Zoe pats Jenny on the head. Jenny placed tenth, which was well above her expectations. She's only a sophomore, and I have a feeling another Brockton Public student might be taking the national scene by storm soon enough.

Jace has remained by my side as I let loose for the first time in far too long. Somehow, things between us are more intimate than ever. We haven't gotten enough of each other this week. His team didn't win the Championship, but it was a very successful season. We've both taken the week off from workouts and instead spent a lot of time together. It's mostly been on Shadow Lane, at his dad's or at my apartment. I know I need to be tough and get over it, but I'm not ready to return to Jace's dorm room yet.

Frankie offered to switch rooms with Jace, but I'm determined to get over my emotional issues. Still in training on that, for now. Soon it will be winter break, and the dorms will be closed for a couple weeks, so I'll have a good excuse to keep holding off on going back there.

Jace leads me away from the crowded living room and into the kitchen. "There's something I've been wanting to tell you all day," he tells me after I hop up on the counter.

"Oh?"

He places his hands on either side of me. Sometimes, when he looks at me like he is right now, I think he might be falling in love all over again. Or maybe that's just me. God, he's beautiful.

"She's expelled from UC, and lost her scholarship. So she's not coming back." He doesn't need to say her name.

"What about the legal charges?" After making my statement to the detective on the case, I wanted nothing to do with it. Or at least, as little as possible. I'm relying on Jace to tell me what I need to know.

"The prosecutor expects she'll probably plead guilty and get some jail time. It's unlikely she'll be found legally crazy, but at the very least, the judge will require some sort of mental treatment as part of her sentence."

I nod, unsure how I feel about this news. It's disturbing that the girl's life is ruined, but she's definitely got some issues. It's just hard to grasp that someone who seemed relatively normal and had so much going for her could be totally unhinged.

"I have something I've been meaning to tell you as well," I say, unable to hide my smugness.

"What would that be?"

"I signed a very important paper this afternoon."

He leans in closer, his lips brushing mine. "What paper?"

"The one that signs me up for four more years in Brockton."

I feel him smile.

It wasn't as easy to make the decision as it would have been years, months or even weeks ago. Love is a powerful thing, but self-preservation is as well. It's not always easy getting what you want, and sometimes it means taking risks. Sometimes it takes patience. And sometimes, I think, as I kiss Jace for the hundredth time that night, it all pays off. Sometimes we get exactly what we want.

Other books in the Pepper Jones series:

Pepped Up (Pepper Jones #1): http://amzn.to/1JZX7Mi

All Pepped Up (Pepper Jones #2): http://amzn.to/1UzlIpL

Pep Talks (Pepper Jones #4): http://amzn.to/1Ph79EI

Pepped Up Forever (Pepper Jones #5): Coming October 2015!

The Pepper Jones Collection (first three books in the series): http://amzn.to/1L2GGVA

Find me online at:

www.alideanfiction.com

www.facebook.com/alideanfiction

www.twitter.com/alideanfiction

www.goodreads.com/author/show/7237069.Ali_Dean

Made in the USA
Middletown, DE
02 September 2015